KYOKO CHURCH

Kyoko Church discovered the power of the written erotic word when she was 16 years old and penned a very explicit missive to her boyfriend detailing all the naughty things she wanted to do to him. When he received it, boyfriend was impressed. When he found it, father was not. For the next 18 years she hid her naughty thoughts in shame until she found a community where they were once again appreciated for the well-imagined smut they are.

A Canuck by birth, she has recently made Australia her home. She is currently learning to drive on the left and say G'day convincingly.

For more naughtiness, follow Kyoko Church on Twitter (@kyokochurch)

ALSO FROM SWEETMEATS PRESS

The Candy Box - Kojo Black
Sun Strokes - Kojo Black
Immoral Views - Various
Named and Shamed - Janine Ashbless
Naked Delirium - Various
Making Him Wait - Kay Jaybee
Seven Deadly Sins - Various
Strummed - Various
Made for Hire - Various
In the Forests of the Night - Vanessa de Sade

Visit www.sweetmeatspress.com

DIARY OF A LIBRARY NERD

◆◆◆◆

KYOKO CHURCH

ILLUSTRATED BY VANITY CHASE

S
SWEETMEATS PRESS

A Sweetmeats Book

First published by Sweetmeats Press 2014

Copyright © Kyoko Church 2014
Illustrations © Vanity Chase 2014

The right of Kyoko Church to be identified as the author of this work
has been asserted by her in accordance with the Copyright, Designs and
Patents Act, 1988

2 4 6 8 10 9 7 5 3 1

ISBN 978-1-909181-70-0

Typeset by Sweetmeats Press
Printed and bound by Lightning Source

Sweetmeats Press
27 Old Gloucester Street, London, WC1N 3XX, England, U. K.
www.sweetmeatspress.com

This book almost didn't happen.

Writing is a funny thing. You need creative spark and energy, you need drive, you need passion, you need time and you need the right space in your head. I had all of those things when I came up with the idea for this book and pitched it to the wonderful folks at Sweetmeats Press, about three years ago now. And then, when it came time for it to be written, I felt like I had none of them. So my first huge thank you goes to Mr. Kojo Black. When I told him my tale of woe he did the virtual equivalent of holding my hand, providing a sympathetic ear and giving me a pat on the back. And when all that was done he said ... we still need our book. It was the kick in the pants I needed.

Thanks go also to the lovely ladies at SARA, the South Australian Romance Writers Association. Writing is a solitary endeavour but when you're not writing it is helpful to be a part of a community. I came into their midst, the new girl with a funny accent who uses more f words and c words in her writing than probably most of them are comfortable with, and still they welcomed me into the fold. Thank you to the wonderful staff at Dymocks Adelaide, particularly Mandy Macky and Louise Fay who, again, gave time to a girl with a funny accent who said she wanted to stand up in their store and use those aforementioned f-words and c-words in front of an audience of their clients. I'm still shocked and impressed they said yes. So evolved the fun and exciting erotica reading event, Sex In Words.

Thank you to my family who will never read this thank you because they will never read this book ... and that is what everyone is comfortable with. Thank you Dawn, my Delia, my rock. I miss our BP nights. Thank you Em. Will I ever stop being like the artist in Miss Jean Brodie?

And to Brett, who gives me love and acceptance ... so I can fly.

—Kyoko Church

DECEMBER **26**

DECEMBER **31**

God, that's bad. No wonder I never finished my BFA.

A portrait of the artist attempting to recapture her youth.

A portrait of the artist as a dried up spinster approaching forty.

A portrait of the artist … because her best friend bought her a sketch pad for Christmas in the desperate attempt to make her care. About something.

Anything.

Happy fucking New Year.

JANUARY 5

I do care about something. Here's the text I got from him today.

I always thought you were beautiful.
Hope it's okay if we stay in touch.

Oh my god, I'm a cougar! No longer am I the geeky spinster who's going to die alone in my house with my seven cats and nobody will find me until someone notices the smell. Now I'm this … .
Maybe I don't care. Because, oh, the things he

makes me think … .

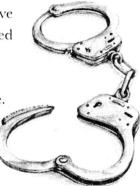

It is not right for me to have these thoughts. Perhaps I need somewhere to purge them.

Yes.

Yes, that's what this will be. A safe haven. A place for no holds barred ranting. A place for secrets.

And drawing. Even if it's bad. Even if it's wrong. No one will see here. No one will see this. This is just for me.

JANUARY 10

Okay, Charlotte, time to take stock.

Current state of affairs in the life of Charlotte Campbell

(God, that sounds pompous … .)

Health: I've always got my health. (I sound like my grandma. Good to start on a high note, though.)

Best friend: The wonderful and ever supportive Delia, my BFF since we were six. (See? Things still okay.)

Creative endeavors: Er, sometimes I draw … stuff. (Moving on!)

Accommodation: Living in my dead father's tiny rundown cottage where he used to come to write his sermons. (Hm, yes, this is where it starts going south.)

Employment: Dead end, repetitious, brainless, monotonous, soul destroying work under the supervision of a tyrannical porcine mutant masquerading as a library technician, the hopelessness of which makes me want to stick pins in a voodoo doll of … someone who shall remain nameless. (Yep. That about says it. Oh wait … .)

Relationship status: Alone. (And therein lies the rub.)

How did it come to this?

JANUARY 17

Pig Face is on the rampage again. As if it's not demoralizing enough to be a grown woman with a tertiary level education whose sole job is to move books from one place to another, Pig Face has to elevate my misery by barking orders at me like I'm Joan Crawford and she's Mommie Dearest.

Every time I come back here you are scribbling in that book … or whatever it is you're doing!

I'm guessing the gimp she must have as a husband failed to get her off again last night since today she's marching around here spewing her wretched bile, like a volcano of rage.

I could tell she's been saving that one up awhile. She's seen me back here ignoring Fritz and working in my sketch pad and she's just been waiting for the time to unload. Yes, I've named the automated book sorter Fritz. It seems appropriate since he's German engineered and always on the fritz. And yes, I am referring to an inanimate object as 'he'. Another indication that keeping me shut away in the bowels of the library, aka The Dungeon, with only a sorter for company will one day steal my sanity. I'll become like that woman who fell in love with the Eiffel Tower. One day Pig Face will come back here and find me making out with Fritz's exception bin or humping his conveyor belt. They'll have to cart me away, raving and mad, and when the poor sap they get to replace me asks why the position is vacant, people will say, "Oh, Charlotte had to go away for a while. We don't talk about Charlotte." To be fair, I know I shouldn't be working on my sketches on the library's dime. But I just get so bored. When all the holds are wrapped and everything's checked in, what else can I do but doodle and ... .

Okay, here's my secret. Well, one of them. A not-so-deep-dark one.

Sometimes I doodle sketches of what I think certain patrons might look like based on the holds that come in for them.

JOHANNESSON,   HENRIETTA loves her romances. At least ten a week come in for her. The odd cookbook, too. About once a month she'll get a different travel book and sometimes the cookbook theme ties in, like that time she ordered *Japan by Rail* and *100 Ramen Recipes*. Somehow I don't think she ever gets to any of the places she reads about.

Then there's **DOBSON, WILLIAM B**. Ostensibly a man of the cloth is Mr. Dobson, mostly requesting non-fiction Christian works by theologians like Thomas Kellerman and C.S. Lewis, or books with titles like, *In Defense of Marriage* or *God's Plan: One Man, One Woman*. But in the last couple of months other non-fic titles have crept in, *How to Open Up Your Marriage* and *Sex at Dawn*. I wonder if old William is merely researching other opinions or if he's planning to spring a Newt Gingrich on the missus. Are all men cheating, lying bastards?

But perhaps that's my skeptical, marriage and religion-weary taint on things.

Then of course there is **CURTIS, NATHAN P**.

Oh, Nathan … .

That's how I ended up here in the first place.

JANUARY **20**

Oh the stuff with Nathan is bad. So bad. Deliciously bad.

It started about two months ago. Before everything went to shit.

Back before I got sent to The Dungeon. Back when I could wear pretty things to work, open toed shoes and nice dresses. When my life made sense, when it was normal and ordered and predictable. When I could talk to people, not just Fritz who doesn't talk back. If he starts to talk back I'll know I'm in trouble.

I'd seen Nathan come in before, mostly to use the computers for those interactive online games, and I never really thought too much about him. He was just some kid into gaming; there are lots of them. But one day something happened that made me notice him. One day, instead of coming in to use the computers, he came in to pick up a hold.

I know now he is eighteen, but he looks younger. He's all legs and arms. His dirty blond hair flops down into his eyes, though thankfully not in that horrid coiffed way that's popular now. Just in an errant, messy way. He's anything but coiffed. His eyes look too big in his face. He has a snub nose and full red lips. His posture is slightly stooped, as though he's not quite sure yet what to do with some recently acquired height.

I wasn't the one processing the holds then, so under normal circumstances I'm sure I never would have found out what book he was getting. He would never have come to the checkout desk with *this* book. He would have scurried over to use the self check, looking over his shoulder to make sure no one saw the cover, and then slipped out of the library as quickly as possible. If that was how it happened that day, maybe our paths would never have intersected the way they did. To me he would continue to be just some kid into gaming, and to him I would be just some woman old enough not to warrant any further consideration.

Although he's since assured me I was never that for him.

But that's not what happened. On this day the self-check station was down. Ah, technology, right? And fate.

Nathan didn't know it was down. He didn't know much of anything about his surroundings on this afternoon. What caught my eye that day was the way he bolted over to the hold shelves with this kind of grim determination, not looking up or around, grabbing his book and then going straight to the self-check, too consumed in his task to notice that no one else was in line there, or the Out of Order sign that was clearly posted.

There I was at the customer service desk with my bright clothes and my cheery 'can I help you' smile (oh, to be cheery again). "I can check you out here," I called, completely unaware of the nature of his hold and the embarrassment it was about to cause. For him. If it were me, I would be embarrassed too. But then that's just the sort of thing that sometimes … turns me on.

It was only then that I saw him notice the Out of Order sign posted on the self-check terminal screen. He looked from the sign to me and then back at the sign again, as though willing it not to be there. The only way I can describe the look in his eyes is ... stricken. For a moment it looked like he was considering whether or not to throw the book down and bolt. I had no idea why. But I was about to find out.

Slowly he dragged himself over to the desk. He placed his book, cover down, in front of me and mumbled something unintelligible while he dug in his wallet for his card.

"Sorry, our self-check station is having a little tantrum this morning," I said, trying to lighten his inexplicably gloomy reaction to being forced to confront a human being for this transaction. I took his card, scanned it through, and plopped his book down on the RFID pad. That's when suddenly everything made sense.

Masturbation: How to Know When Your Habit Has Become an Addiction, popped up on my screen.

I take my job seriously (or I did, when my job wasn't a joke). I see all manner of things being checked out and, particularly for non-fiction items, I try and mind my own business. I am friendly and chatty if it seems a person is open to that. But often when someone has stacks of books I don't even notice what I'm putting through. I am courteous and professional. Normally. But not this day.

A chuckle escaped me. A little guffaw from the back

of my throat.

I slapped my hand over my mouth and immediately remembered myself. I looked away, cleared my throat and quickly switched screens, printing the checkout receipt. It wouldn't have gone any further than that, really it wouldn't have. I would have just given him his receipt and off he would have gone. Except.

Except that as I handed him his receipt our eyes met briefly. Our fingers touched. A frisson went through me as my hand connected with his hand and our eyes locked. He looked mortified … and yet. I saw something else. Something pleading. Something dark and submissive. Something in him that enjoyed that brief moment where I saw his weakness. Which made an evil little spark in me light up.

A very evil little spark indeed.

JANUARY 22

So I met Delia for lunch yesterday. She wanted to talk about ... him. HWSNBN. He Who Shall Not Be Named.

I told her I don't see what the big fucking deal is. We're split, he's gone, it's over. Finished. Done. What is the point in talking about it? It's not like we will ever be getting back together. I mean, obviously. Could it be any more fucking obvious? Anymore humiliatingly obvious?

Moving on, that's what I have to do, what I have to focus on. I need to concentrate on things like ... getting my life back to looking like something I actually recognize as *my life*. I mean, where did that go? How does a person go from marriage, beautiful house, two cars, weekly dinners out, vacations every year ... to ... whatever the fuck this is. Living in a run down shack. Working in The Dungeon. Chained to Fritz. Fantasizing about someone half my age.

I told her, Dee, I don't need to talk about HWSNBN. "You're obviously still in pain, Char," she said. Pain, shmain. "You can't even say his name." I can say his name. I simply choose not to. There's a difference.

Eventually she gave up on this line of questioning and went back to regaling me with stories from Shady Oaks Nursing Home where she works as the charge nurse. Mr. Peabody flushed his dentures down the toilet. Again. "He thinks he's washing them!" Mrs. Del Rizzo got caught in bed with Mr. Goodfellow while Mrs. Goodfellow was at bingo. "She's a horny old bat." Then there were stories of

Sebastian and the kids. Missy got loose and fell down the stairs at the cottage last week. Sebastian got that job at the school in town. He doesn't have to travel outside the city anymore.

You might think that I would be jealous of Dee. Sebastian is the perfect husband. Kind and smart and, oh my god, so fucking sexy, not to mention totally in love with Delia. They have two gorgeous kids, Miles and Missy. I should be jealous, even more now, considering the state of things. Maybe I would be if she were any other person, any other kind of friend. But Delia's my rock. She's seen me through the worst times.

"How about your sketching?" she asked before we left.

"My sketching is crap, thanks for asking."

"Char … ."

"Seriously, Dee. The last thing I gave any serious time to was a self portrait that is so laughable I want to do a Van Gogh and cut my ear off. Or maybe my hand. How about you? Did you submit to that gallery last week?"

"I did. I'm not holding my breath."

"Your stuff is brilliant, Dee, nothing like the crap I do. Was it the watercolor of the rain forest? They're blind if they don't take that."

"It was. I don't know if it's what they're looking for, though," she said as we were walking out. "And you don't give your work enough credit. It's really good too, Char. Really good."

If she only knew what I've been drawing lately ... .

JANUARY 26

I don't think it's right that the entire library staff knows when Pig Face is in one of her moods. The moment I walked in today I heard it from everyone. *Watch out for Sue. It's a nasty one today.* And then everyone's gotta be on egg shells. I'll just hide in The Dungeon with Fritz and hope that she has enough with the front line staff to keep her occupied. Maybe someone will put a Blu-ray on the DVD cart and provoke a five-minute lecture about Everything In Its Place.

Maybe I'll hear from Nathan.

The day after the masturbation book incident he came back in and skulked around, hovering around the edges of the library. He did that for a few days. He would sit at a computer for a while but not really do any gaming. Mostly he'd mess around on social media before he'd appear restless and then get up and pace around the WWII section of non-fiction, picking up books and glancing at them before putting them back in the wrong places. I'd trail behind him, not too closely, re-shelving everything properly lest it incur the wrath of Pig Face.

It was while I was involved in this re-shelving, one eye on the books, one eye out to see where he'd gone, that Nathan suddenly appeared from the opposite direction that I'd been looking.

"Check this out," he said.

He was holding his phone out and his Twitter app was open. There was a picture of a book and an apple with the caption 'A book a day keeps reality away' across it.

"Cute," I said.

"Are you on Twitter?" Nathan asked.

"Not a lot."

"You should follow me," he said. "WarGod207."

"Charming," I said. I looked back at the picture on his phone. "And what reality are you trying to keep away?" I asked it innocently enough. But the way we were looking at each other, I knew that book he checked out was there between us. So I added, "Is your book helping?"

What was it about the kid? I'd never acted that way before. I knew I was toying with him but I could hardly help it. I felt like a cat with a mouse.

Now that I'm stuck in the Dungeon and never get out into the stacks to see him it just gives me more time to … to what? To think about him. To fantasize. Hmmm … .

Oh, to think of him, so innocently concerned about his onanistic pursuits. Part of me wants to comfort him, to whisper in his ear, "It's okay, sweet boy, there's nothing wrong with you. It's normal. A normal, healthy thing for you to do." But then another part of me rises, a darker part. I still want to whisper those things but all while I wrap my own hand around his eager cock. "Aw, does that feel good? You like when I do that, don't you?"

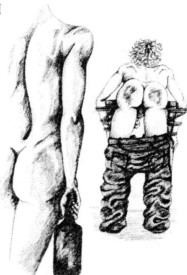

Then as I stroke him, as he gets close, that dark part of me wants to chastise him for being such a naughty, horny boy.

January 27

A black day. No working. No sketching. No eating or talking.

Just sleeping.

Had that dream again. The one where Dee and I are in trouble for talking in church while daddy is preaching and he makes us scrub the pews.

I hate that dream.

January 24

I'm not scheduled to work today. About an hour ago Delia called me and wanted to know how things have been going since … well, since I was sent to The Dungeon. I told her it's fine. "I move material around, I sketch when it's quiet, I try and avoid Pig Face, I come home."

I didn't mention Nathan. I can tell Dee most anything but that stuff, those things I think are just weird. And the sketches. Well, I could never show anybody those.

"And how is it, staying at the cottage?" she asked.

"Good. Fine. I mean, thank god I have this place."

"You know you could have come here."

"Dee, things are busy enough at your place. Missy and Miles don't need dreary old Auntie Char moping around. And I'd probably just try and shag Sebastian when you weren't looking."

"I'm sure he'd oblige."

"Yeah, right. You've got the only good one, my friend."

"Yes well," she paused. "If it ever gets to be too lonely, or too, you know, weird for you at your dad's cottage you know you can stay here."

"Thanks," I said. We were quiet a moment.

"Char, are you ever going to tell me what happened at work?" I felt my face go hot and I didn't answer. "Come on Char, it's me. You can tell me anything. Why did they put you back in the sorter room?"

"I will tell you, Dee," I finally said. "Next time I see you."

FEBRUARY 1

Sometimes the monotony of this place gets to me more than usual. Like now, I'm into the seventh hour of a mind numbing eight-hour shift. I'm ready to poke my eyes out from the boredom. The public throws books into Fritz.

Fritz sorts them into bins. I take them out. I put them on carts. Out they go to the public. They bring them back to Fritz. And on and on and on. All I do is shuffle books and movies from one place to another.

Thank god for Melody. She's the only one who visits me back here.

I was just about to ask Fritz what he's doing for dinner later when Melody's shiny black bob appeared in the doorway. "Hey Charlotte!" she said. "Your boy toy is picking up a hold."

"He's not my boy toy, Mel, gawd." Then I thought, Nathan's picking up a hold? He hadn't done that since the masturbation book incident, as far as I was aware. His last text to me had been relatively brief.

> When are they letting you out of there? I loved that sexy little black and white dress you always wore. The book's not working.

I'd texted back.

> Maybe I should make you check out other books. More embarrassing ones.

"Want me to stake it out?" Melody said. She was grinning like a mad woman.

"Don't let Sue catch you!" (I try not to call her Pig Face out loud.)

Five minutes later Mel was back.

"He couldn't check out. Didn't have the card. I nabbed the hold for you." She handed me a DVD. *To Kill a Mockingbird.* The hold slip read HARDEN, EDWARD.

"This isn't his," I said to Mel.

"It was what he was trying to check out."

I went to the computer and pulled up the account for HARDEN, EDWARD. It was a virtual account that was set up online two days ago.

Wait a second. Harden? Mockingbird?

Got it. Nathan.

I looked up the other holds on the account. I was not prepared for how my body would react when I read the titles.

BDSM, Beyond the Basics. Domination: Your Guide to Becoming a Master. Playing Well: Exploring Kink.

All the air went out of my lungs. My leg started to jiggle up and down on its own. I felt hot. It was Nathan. From my seat I looked up at Mel standing beside me but she was still staring at the screen. I swallowed and took a breath.

"It's okay. I'll handle this." I looked up the email address for the account and composed a letter while Melody read over my shoulder.

Dear Mr. Harden,

Thank you for your recent online registration. Please note that to activate your account you must visit the library with proper identification verifying your existence.

"Verifying your existence?" Mel said. "Charlotte,

what are you doing?"

I tried to giggle but it came out a raspy kind of choke. "Mel, don't you see? Mocking? Harden? Nathan set up this account. He's messing with me. Or he has books he wants to check out that he's too embarrassed to have in his own name. You saw what the other holds were. Or it's both. Either way ... " I turned back to my email.

> Until you can do so, your *Mocking* hold will be held for you for one week. You will be notified by email when your other interesting choices in reading material arrive. Which, again, you will not be able to check out without proper ID.
>
> Customer Service
> Parkdale Library

I hit Send. Then I did a search in the catalogue. I found a book called *On Being a Good Submissive*. I placed my find on hold for HARDEN, EDWARD and Mel gasped.

"Charlie," Mel said low. "Haven't you gotten into enough trouble here recently?"

I sighed. "It's no big deal. Nathan's having a little fun with me, I'm having a little fun with him, it's all just a bit of nonsense to pass the time. Lord knows I gotta do something to keep my brain from shriveling up in here." I spun around in my chair and grinned at her while I thought about Nathan checking his email and finding this message and his new hold.

I thought about Nathan the whole way home from work. The books he put on hold! Oh my god. Those books. I can't believe it. I can't believe what he's thinking. Oh god, what this means. What this means could be possible between us. Maybe I could show him my drawings. Maybe he would like them. Maybe he'd even be turned on. Maybe he'd think they were good.

But I can't. Not after what happened the last time someone saw a drawing of mine like that.

Besides have I gone completely mad? He's 18. He's barely an adult. Last week he checked out a whole season of *Dragon Ball Z*. Whatever flirting we've done in the past, however he looks at me, whatever my dirty mind conjures up, there cannot really be anything between us.

Even after what happened in the bathroom.

FEBRUARY 3

LEVITT, HENRY *30 Ways to Improve Your Marriage.*

This is the hold I just shelved. I want to scream at this patron. Ha! What a fucking joke. Don't even bother. Marriage is an archaic institution that has no place in the modern world. We weren't meant to pair bond with one person forever. Doesn't everybody know that by now? Why are we continuing this charade? One man, one woman, riding off into the sunset, happily ever after, that is nonsense that Disney insidiously plants in young minds, that the church needs us to believe, that society seems to rely upon. I want to open this LEVITT, HENRY's account and put *The Myth of Monogamy* on hold for him. But I don't need any more trouble here at work.

LEVITT, HENRY. I wonder about him. How old is he? Has he cheated? Thought about it? Or maybe it's his wife who's been unfaithful. Maybe he's the one who's trying to hold things together. It's making a burny feeling start in my chest. MRS. LEVITT, HENRY doesn't appreciate him. Here is a man who is at least looking for answers. At least he's trying. What I would have given to have seen a little effort.

I was always the one trying with Bill HWSNBN. The one to say, this isn't working. The one looking up the self help books. The one to make appointments with counselors and therapists. "At least he's agreed to go," is what Delia said at the time. I thought, yes, that's true, as I sat in yet another office set up in someone's basement, a cramped room with a couch, a bookcase, a desk and a computer, certificates hanging on the wall. At least he's here with me.

I'd talk. He'd listen. Or at least he did a reasonable impression of someone listening, I think now. He'd answer the therapist's questions too. We would leave after the hour having gotten exactly … nowhere. We'd go back to our life. Our life of "what's on TV tonight." Of "what do you want for dinner." Of "I have an early morning tomorrow, I'm going to bed. No, that's fine, you stay up and finish watching your show." A life where I routinely went to bed alone, aching and lonely. A life where I had a roommate instead of a husband. A life of tedium, the desperation of which left me alternately feeling like I was trying with all my might to punch my way out of a rubber sack and like I was slowly sinking into the sea, a water logged body, in a way that was almost beautiful in its floaty submission of will, like the opposite of flying, arms splayed out and falling into the murky depths.

Marriage. What a fucking joke.

Nathan just texted me!

> I miss you. The view in the library
> isn't nearly as beautiful without you.

Oh, to be beautiful in someone's eyes! My stomach is filled with a shimmery sensation. No mention of the books on hold or my email though. Should I follow suit?

> Trust me, the view in the sorter room
> ain't pretty either. Did you bring
> proper ID into the library today?

He just responded: Lol.

Hmm.

And yes, I'm texting with someone who uses lol. And the worst part? Now *I* use lol.

Here's the thing with lol. I used to hate it. I used to judge anyone who used it. I admit it. I judged. I was an lol-ist. An lol-ophobe.

I hated the falseness of it. When you type lol every other sentence, you are not lol-ing. Nobody lols that much. Not people outside mental institutions, anyway.

But then Nathan happened. And I did a whole if-you-can't-beat-em-join-em thing. And soon enough I was lol-ing with the best of them. I started using lol even when I was texting other people, not just Nathan.

Because, I finally realized, everyone knows you aren't lol-ing when you type lol. It's just a softener. It's three little letters that say, 'don't take what I just typed too seriously.'

My marriage is a joke. Lol.

I'm so depressed. Lol.

Oh god, just kill me now. Lol.

You see? You see how that works? It's actually a very useful little acronym. I just love it. Lol.

FEBRUARY 6

At work today there was a response from Nathan to the email I sent about his hold.

> Thank you for your email. I apologize, I should have realized I would need to visit the library with identification to check out my book. Unfortunately I am not able to get there for a while. Are you able to extend my hold until February 19th?
> As for my choices in reading material … I'm glad you find them interesting.
> Edward Harden

He was so funny! What little game was he playing at now? I wondered if there was a reason for February 19th.

I wrote back.

Dear Mr. Harden,

Are you asking for me to bend the library's rules to suit your timetable? Normally I am not able to do so but since there are no other patrons waiting for *Mockingbird* and since you are such a loyal patron of the library I suppose I can do it this once. However, I note that if you are going to continue to ask for special favors in the future we may have to come to some sort of arrangement, a barter agreement, if you will. I will leave you to think about what you might be able to offer.

My heart was racing. I grinned wickedly at Fritz and gave him a wink. But then I hesitated a moment. I had glimmers of that same feeling I had the day I found out about HWSNBN, the same day of the incident with Nathan. Considering the despair I was in, I remembered musing over the irony of what an amazing feeling it was. When the life you're used to is ripped away it is devastating. But there is also an element of freedom, a feeling that if this could happen then what else really matters? And if nothing really matters then you can do anything. It is a big feeling, powerful and breathtaking. In the midst of my despair I also felt like I could fly.

But look where that got me. Now I'm like a caged bird.

I shook my head. No. Caged was what I was before. This was the new Charlotte, the single Charlotte, the Charlotte who could chat and flirt and who uses lol. Who took risks. Who engaged a boy half her age in sexual banter. I went back to my email.

Please ask at the desk for your hold.

But then I stopped. If Pig Face or really anyone other than Melody is on desk when Nathan comes up to inquire about a special hold and they caught wind it was something I'd done it could be more trouble. I deleted that sentence.

If you require any further suggestions for reading material I am always happy to recommend titles. In fact you may have noticed I have taken the liberty of putting another title on hold, something perhaps more suited to you. Although you seem to have done well thus far searching out material to help you with your issues.

I giggled thinking of the book I'd found before, *On Being a Good Submissive*, and contemplating how I might make it clear that I am using 'issue' as a double entendre. I even looked it up. Issue: Discharge. Emission. Lol! But I decided it was enough as it was.

I held my breath. And clicked Send.

Not two minutes later and he'd responded!

I'm sorry, I didn't realize extending my hold would be considered a "special favor". But if you feel a barter arrangement is in order I may be able to comply.
May I ask who I'm emailing with? It will help me in suggesting an appropriate offering.

Cute. Very cute. I decided to play along.

This is Charlotte, goddess of the automated sorter and knower of all holds placed at the Parkdale Library.

But then, you already know that. I look forward to your
suggestion.

I sent it quickly and stared at my inbox, willing
another message to come through. Instead Pig Face came
in and caught me staring dreamily at my screen.

She glanced at the boxes of delivery material I had
yet to put through Fritz and barked at me about how it had
to get done before the evening shift. What was annoying
about this was a) it doesn't. The evening person would
be even more bored than usual if there were no delivery
material left to process. And b) who the hell died and
left her to rule her tyrannical biblio-realm? This was the
library, not a widget manufacturing plant. There were no
quotas to make, no deadlines. No one would die if they
didn't get their hold until tomorrow. Geez.

There was a time when I thought the library was a
fun place to work.

Pig Face left and I turned back to my email. Lo
and behold there was another message from Nathan's fake
account.

Nice to 'meet' you, Charlotte. A Goddess, huh? Hm. Since
you find the items I currently have on hold "interesting",
perhaps my offer can be to discuss your interest in them?
Do you have experience in the lifestyle?

Yes 'meet,' in quotations. Like we hadn't met
before. But whoa! Experience? Lifestyle? Nathan was full
of surprises today. That excited feeling crept back into

me, I felt flushed with it. I glanced back through some of my drawings. A tiny part of me wanted to tell him about them, show him. But what did I say? I was like some 19th century cad: *Why don't you come up and see my etchings.* God. He asked about experience. Was reading everything about Dom/sub play I could find on the net and sketching out my lurid fantasies considered experience? It was just a passing interest, really. More of an ... anthropological pursuit. It's compelling to know what other people get up to in bedroom. But lifestyle? What could he, an 18-year-old boy, know about 'the lifestyle,' as he put it?

For some reason all my bravado and desire for banter deflated. I felt small and I just wanted to be plain.

No experience. But I have an active imagination.

No other replies came after that. Now my shift is almost over and I have the next couple of days off. Tonight I am looking forward to an evening of eating cold leftover pizza and trying not to think about HWSNBN and what he might be doing at home, in our house, with ... well, I'm trying not to think of it. Sometimes I imagine telling Fritz. "My life sucks," I'd say mournfully. He'd sigh and spit a book into his exception bin in commiseration, as if to say, sometimes I can't take what people throw at me either.

FEBRUARY 11

It's been a bad night.

Delia and I usually try and meet for lunch or dinner about once a month. Although our quick lunch last month didn't give us time for our usual deep and meaningfuls. Also there hadn't been any wine. Wine is key.

So we went to Gino's. We always go to Gino's, this little local Italian place. We start off saying we'll just order salad, maybe some bruschetta. I know watching your weight is archaic and anti feminist and totally buying into the damaging social messages we put out there, particularly to girls. Dee and I are both (relatively) mature, educated women and should know better. But Dee says she's always wanted to be described as 'lithe'. "Mm, yes, lithe," I said dreamily. My word is 'slip', as in, 'she's a slip of a girl'. We talk about how many kilometers we've managed to run that week, running being the mostly hated but effective weight maintenance activity for both of us. All those kilometers we've put in, surely that deserves more than a little salad, we say, although I mostly fudge my numbers and suspect Delia does the same. In the end we always say "screw it" and order the big panzerotti and fries that we both know we wanted to begin with.

"Okay," Dee said once the waiter had set our plates down, each with a huge, steaming doughy pocket atop it that emitted a gorgeous spicy tomato scent. "You've finally got to tell me what happened at work. What got you landed in the back with the sorter? Did you finally snap and yell at that pig person you're always complaining about?"

"Pig Face," I said and Dee snorted out a chuckle. "Exactly." I smirked at the noise.

"Stop stalling, Char. Damn, are you really that

afraid to just tell me?

"I'm telling, I'm telling," I said.

So I took a big gulp of rich red wine and I explained to Delia about the book Nathan was checking out the day the self-check was down. She chuckled. "Poor kid," she said. And then I told her about how he approached me with his Twitter app. "Then I mentioned the book again." I told her.

"Why did you do that?" Dee asked, looking genuinely confused.

At this point I had to make a decision. I could have glossed over the details of what happened, shrugged a lot and been vague, blamed the outcome on Pig Face being on yet another rampage. It wasn't much of a decision, really. While the latter is perfectly conceivable, the vagaries and avoidance tactics would never fly with Delia. She would have kept probing to get the whole truth out of me sooner or later. I figured I might as well save her the trouble. The problem is … how can I explain it? I barely understand it myself.

"It was the day I walked in on, you know … them. He Who Shall Not—"

"I got it. Bill and—"

I grimaced and Dee stopped talking. "I wasn't myself. And you had to see this kid when he was checking out that book, Dee. He looked so … small. Meek. Desperate."

There are other things about the way he looked. His dirty blond, unkempt hair, his unruly body, like he'd just recently gone from skinny boy to the beginnings of the muscled body of the man he'd soon be, those insanely full, red lips that were almost feminine and those deer in headlight eyes. There was a naked insecurity in those eyes, mixed with the slightly hard edge borne of rejection. The turmoil that appeared to go on in his head was infinitely interesting and alluring to me. "When I mentioned the book to him the next day, all of those same qualities were painted all over his face again. It just, it triggered something in me."

"You wanted to help him?" Dee offered.

"Sort of," I said. I paused. "Not exactly." I felt my face flush with heat.

Delia looked at me with the same expression I saw her use last week when Miles decided to stick his slice of bologna on his sister's bum while she was running around naked. Bewildered. "Why don't you just keep telling me what happened," she said slowly.

I looked down. "We ended up having this conversation about it." I shrugged. "About masturbation."

"Right there in the—"

"Yep," I said, trying not to look as ashamed as I then felt. I thought of how Nathan looked that day, staring into his lap. "I kind of do that a lot," he'd said, sitting in one of the private study carrels in the back. He spoke so softly I had to draw up one of the nearby chairs to lower myself closer to him and hear. He let out a "ha" like he was trying to lighten the tone of the confession, but it didn't really work. I remember being surprised. I didn't think someone his age would have that worry, thought all that hairy palm nonsense was way behind us. But who knew how he'd grown up?

"Oh yeah?" I said. I wanted to smile but he looked so serious. "Like, how much is a lot?"

"Like, a couple times a day."

I didn't say anything.

"Okay, more like five or six."

I did smile then, let out a chuckle. But the poor thing just cringed and shrank down.

"Aw, it's okay, sweetie" I said, and I remembered not knowing where the tone in my voice came from. It was unlike any I'd used before, all dripping and syrupy. "Really." And this I said with as much sincerity as I could. "It's just your body exercising its biological imperative."

He looked up at me then. "Yeah?" He even managed a weak smile. "Biological?"

"Yeah," I said, tucking both hands under my thighs, suddenly aware how close to him I was sitting. "You know, procreate or die? You're healthy."

"Healthy," he said, then paused. His eyes lowered and his voice got so quiet again I had to lean forward and strain to hear. "Are ... are you healthy too?"

He was looking at me so intently. I'd never had anyone stare at me with such naked lust. I glanced at his lap and noticed a bulge. He saw me looking at it and squirmed.

That's   when   that   I   suddenly   remembered

HWSNBN. Flashes of my discovery that morning assaulted me for what felt like the millionth time that day. I felt angry and reckless and free. That big, scary, jumping-off-a-cliff feeling.

Nathan continued looking at me in a way no one had before, boy or man. A smile unfurled across my face, like I was the Cheshire cat, a wide, flirty grin. I don't know what possessed me, other than that reckless feeling. But the next thing we were in the women's bathroom, the one at the back of the building that needed a staff key and was out of order eleven months out of twelve. I had one leg on the floor of the stall, the other on the toilet seat, blouse unbuttoned, skirt pushed up, panties pulled to the side. Nathan had his back against   the   sink,   staring into the stall, mouth agape, a pantomime of disbelief as he stared at my fingers working furiously against my aching clit.

"You   brought him with you into the bathroom?" Dee was incredulous.   "And Pig Face walked in?"

"That   woman can sniff out dissension in the ranks anywhere in the building."

"Char, what in the hell were you thinking? You could have been fired."

"I wish I had been," I said. "It would be better than still having to go there everyday."

"Stop it. You love the library."

"Loved. Past tense."

"You don't mean that." Dee looked like a child who'd just been told there was no Santa. "Charlotte, I know what's happened with Bill has thrown you, but you can't go messing up the rest of your life because your marriage didn't work out. What could you possibly want with a guy so young?"

How do I explain it to Dee? How can I tell her that his innocence, his naïveté, that look he gives me all filled with naked, untapped lust awakens something in me. Something scary. Something I don't know if I want to acknowledge. It feels like a beast slumbering beneath the surface of my calm exterior. Delia, married to the sexy Sebastian who completely satisfies her in bed, with her beautiful children and her inspired watercolor paintings of endangered animals. As much as I love her and know she loves me, I just cannot reveal the depravity I feel lurking, that has been building for years.

What I've finally begun to unleash.

You can't imagine what Dee said next.

"You should talk to him, Char."

"Yeah?" I said, surprised and excited. "You think I should text Nathan right now?" I asked, pulling out my phone.

"No," she said. "Bill."

I just stared at her at first. I almost laughed. "You must be joking."

"He called Sebastian—"

"He called Sebastian??" I sputtered. "What did he say? Did you talk to him? Oh my god, I can't believe him."

"He feels terrible, Char. He's worried about you."

"Motherfucker."

I want to note something here. It's about swearing. I never used to swear. Never really felt the need to. Swearing was something other people did, people who probably didn't read enough books, I used to feel, whose vocabulary wasn't extensive enough for them to access the words they actually wanted to use so they just cursed instead.

What I didn't understand was the intense satisfaction that comes from spitting out the most crude, foul word you can think of to match the bile and rage you feel at being so egregiously wronged by the person in your life who has pledged to love you. So yes, at this point in my conversation with Dee I did say "motherfucker." I said it nice and slowly. Mo-ther-fuck-er. I loaded each syllable with all the disdain and disgust I could muster.

"He's worried about me? He wasn't too worried about me the day I found him with that fucking slut." Mm, those last two words were enjoyable to say too.

"You know that's not exactly fair. You told me you spoke to Ashley about it first."

I felt like she'd punched me.

I stood.

"Char, sit down. I'm not saying this to hurt you. I'm not excusing what he did. But," she looked at me cautiously, "you know, if you're going to play with fire … ."

Tears sprung to my eyes. I felt a horrible, oppressive shroud of shame envelop me. I felt strangled by the unfairness of it.

"Oh Charlotte, I'm sorry, I didn't mean—"

I cleared my throat and pulled my things together. "No. It's fine, Dee. It's just fine." I looked down at her. "It's just fine that my best friend thinks it's my fault that my husband was fucking around on me."

She called after me, I heard her shouting for me to stay as I walked away. But I needed away from there, from that conversation.

I knew the conversation I wanted to be having.

FEBRUARY 13

It's not really my fault. It's just that my fight with Delia brought that reckless feeling again. And I gave in. I gave in last night to the desire to contact Nathan.

I told myself initially that it would just be a simple text or two. I just wanted to know if he was still thinking of me. But one and two lead to three and four and soon the texts were flying between us, fast and furious. Since I don't have to work today I let myself stay up all night toying with him via text, a pillow between my legs and a million vivid scenarios in my head.

Nathan, for his part, has been texting a torrent of pent up passion. All of his fantasies, his sweet, sweet fantasies that surprise me with their romance. Aren't boys his age supposed to be surly and jaded? Aren't they supposed to be tainted by video games and porn and reduced to taking all vowels out of words when they text? He is not. He spells out words, uses complete sentences and those sentences describe elaborate dreams of passionate unions. He's desperate to know how it will look, feel, sound, smell, taste when he melds his body into another's, when he "becomes one," as he says, with the girl of his dreams.

> **Desperate to know? Haven't you done it before?**

I texted it quickly, before I had the chance to change my mind. When my phone buzzed with the response I closed my eyes a moment to savor the breathy feeling of anticipation before I looked at how he'd answered.

> **No. Never.**

Never. Oh.

A virgin.

I had an angel on one shoulder who was moony eyed over the beautiful innocence of his words, while the devil on my other rubbed her hands together with glee.

> **Let me watch you again.**

I gulped when I read the text.

Watch me?

I was pretty sure I knew what he meant.

Like before. In the bathroom.

I paused, not knowing how to continue, but his next text came blasting through.

Come on.
It's not like I haven't already seen
you do it. Please.

I thought about Delia, our fight. I thought about her asking what the heck I was doing, about what I could possibly want with someone so young.

Nathan this isn't right. I shouldn't
have done that. And you should
be spending time with a girl your
own age. You can do all your
experimenting together.

But his response came right away again.

I don't care about our ages. I'm an
adult and so are you. I don't want
to experiment. I want someone who
knows to show me.

There was barely a pause and then ... .

Charlotte

I was alarmed by his sudden use of my name.

> I want to know how you pleasure
> yourself.

The fact that he said it like that, used those words, I felt something loosen inside me, something that had been bound up tight for years.

> I want to know so that I can be the
> one to do it for you.

My angel was chirping away about how I should leave Nathan to have the experiences he was supposed to with some nice little girl he knew from school named Brittany who had posters in her locker of the latest boy band and had a part time job as a lifeguard after school. But the devil. Oh the devil in me had things to say too.

> Please Charlotte. Why won't you
> show me how to please you?

Oh god. I want to do things to you, I imagined texting him. All your little comments and charming self-deprecations about your inexperience coupled with your open-mindedness. Your obvious willingness to learn. To please. God, how it makes my brain whir and stew and conjure. I want to take you. To make you. Make you my own.

Wouldn't he run screaming if he knew the depraved things that the alluring combination of innocence and eager curiosity invoke in me? All the lurid fantasies I've had. Not just making. Forcing. Restraining. Making him beg. Making him suffer. And then denying him over and over. The idea of pitting his neediness against him makes me burn bright with evil, carnal plans.

Lying there in my bed, alone and wet, wanting and, for a change, wanted, it was all I could do not to text him and tell him to meet me here at my little cottage where I could show him all the things he so desperately wants to know, that I so desperately want to teach him.

But I didn't.

> Nathan, I'm sorry.
> This is just wrong.

Dee's right about one thing. I don't know what the heck I'm doing.

But for now at least I've turned off my phone. It's time to go to sleep.

February 14

Valentine's Day.
Whatever.

February 17

When I got in to work this morning and checked my emails there was one from Nathan's fake account. After the heat and tension of our text exchange the other day I almost forgot about the silly little email banter we had going. When I saw it I remembered, the last thing I said was that I had an active imagination.

> I would think the library is a good place for a person with an active imagination to work. Although it seems a shame for someone as intriguing as yourself to be limited to processing book requests. Do you have other duties there? Or is it because you're bored that you've resorted to taking such a keen interest in the library customers' extra curricular reading material?

I checked the time stamp on the email and noticed it came in after I left for home that day, in other words, much before our recent steamy texts. But considering how I ended that texting session, I really shouldn't encourage him. I should simply ignore this message.

Then my phone buzzed. My heart lurched as I saw 'HWSNBN' come up. (Yes, I've changed his name on my phone to come up 'HWSNBN'. Perhaps that's stupid and immature. The old Charlotte would have thought so. But for the new Charlotte it stops her from wanting to smash her smart phone into teeny tiny pieces like the way she wanted to the first time she saw 'Bill Lewis calling' after she discovered him doing ... what he was doing ... with Ashley.) I quickly clicked my phone off and turned to email. I thought of Nathan's BDSM books on hold.

> I only take "such a keen interest" when the subject matter is so deliciously naughty.

The reckless feeling swelled in my chest as I hit Send. A reply came quickly.

> So let's see. A bored library worker with an active imagination, an interest in all things naughty and an

apparent sharp wit. Sounds like a recipe for trouble.

Oh right. As if he didn't know just how much
trouble. As if he wasn't aware of where our bathroom
encounter landed me!

Ha ha ha. No need to rub it in.

I was about to send this one as swiftly as the others.
But then I smirked at my good buddy Fritz and added
something.

Then again, I know you are good at rubbing.

I peered around me, making sure Pig Face was
nowhere in sight, then glanced back to my email, willing a
response to come.

Do you, now? And what are you good at?

My pulse quickened. The recklessness in me
wanted to tell him I'm good at certain touching too. Part
of me wanted to confess that last night, even though I had
enough will power to refrain from inviting him into my bed
in reality, my fantasies were a different story. My fingers
had teased between my legs while I'd thought thoughts of
Nathan, of being his first, of teaching him things, of going
beyond anything he's thought of in those sweet fantasies
he's texted, of going somewhere dark. First I'd used my
fingers and then I'd used my bullet vibe and when I was
finally sated I'd lost count of how many times I'd frigged
myself over the edge thinking of a boy who—when I said

my favorite singer in high school was Huey Lewis—said, "Who's Huey Lewis?"

I'm good at lots of things. I'm sure I could teach you a thing or three.

I gleefully anticipated what he'd have to say to that.

The truly wise among us know we are never done learning. I'm sure there are things I could teach a saucy little minx like yourself as well.

God, the balls Nathan had on him when he was corresponding via email! Yet I could not deny what his tone did to me. When I thought of those innocent eyes and sweet fantasies my body felt injected with a surge of power, a desire to own and control him. But the email version of him made me feel giggly and girly.

I heard Pig Face's voice from down the hall then so I minimized my email and began my daily routine of emptying Fritz's various bins. Now things are quiet and I can't decide. Sketch or check mail?

WEDNESDAY, FEBRUARY 18

FITZSIMMONS, GRACE *Fifty Shades Darker*

When I put that hold on the cart earlier today I rolled my eyes. In the staff room before we opened, Mel was complaining about Mrs. Fitzsimmons.

"'This *Fifty Shades* book has so much foul language and disgusting depravity in it,' the old cow said to me. 'It's completely disgusting.' And she's looking at me like it's my fault. Like *I* wrote the damned thing. She was so pissed off," Mel said.

"Personally, I think she loves it," I told Mel. "She loves being able to throw her moral outrage at you."

"You're probably right," Mel said. "But why does she have to be so accusing? Then she started in about her fines. 'I wasn't notified they were due! Now you're expecting me to pay for being assaulted by those words!' she said. God, can you believe her? And it's always me she does this with. She would never pull this stuff with Sue. I feel like her punching bag."

"Fucking people," I said. And I meant it. People. They were the worst.

You know, I don't know why I'm complaining about being in the Dungeon with Fritz. Yes, he's temperamental. Yes, occasionally a book will get lodged in his conveyor belt, one of those skinny early readers, and I have to shut him down, crawl in and fish it out. But I can deal with that. At least he's not people.

◆◆◆◆

I have to call Delia. I need her advice. She was right. I don't know what I'm doing. I'm still taking risks here at work but I feel helpless to stop.

I was writing that last entry when there was a knock on the outside door of the sorter room. It's the staff entry door that opens around the side of the building. Staff who enter from there have key card access and if they forget their card there is a bell. So no one ever knocks. When I hesitantly opened the door, who should be standing there but Nathan.

When did the switch in my brain flip? When did I give up denying the inevitability of giving in to what I wanted, regardless of what my sane self or Dee or anyone told me was right? Maybe it was when I let him wordlessly pull me outside into the alley, the door closing heavily behind us. Maybe it was when he said, "Charlotte, please help me. I can't stop thinking about you. I'm hard all the time." Or maybe it was when I pressed myself against him, pressed him up against the brick wall of the building, pressed the lower part of my belly snug against his crotch and felt that, indeed, he was hard, straining against his jeans. Maybe. But really, now that I think about it, there's no question. I know exactly when it was.

I reached up and threaded my hands into that tousled mop of his dirty blond hair. He smelled of mint and cheap cologne and something else underneath, smells of a boy masquerading as a man. I pulled his lips close to mine but didn't kiss him. He was breathing hard, his eyes shiny and round, full of wonder and lust. I could tell he was waiting but he didn't know what for, tense and eager, desperate, a slave to all the hormones raging inside of him. The feel of his shaft pulsing against me and that look that said he was giving himself over to me completely made me wet with the power of it. I felt my starved pussy clench and moisten with the potency of being at the centre of all of his lust filled attention. The top button of my blouse had come undone in the shifting of our bodies and he was staring down at the full round curves of the tops of my breasts. I pressed my arms in on either side of them, making my cleavage more pronounced, pushing the flesh up at his hungry eyes, and he groaned.

"Oh god, Charlotte, please," he said, and I knew then I would get addicted to that desperate, pleading tone in his voice.

"You want me to help you?" I whispered, staring up at him. "You need me to help you get control of your pathetic little urges?" As I said it, I put my hand between us and cupped the hard flesh I felt beneath his jeans. His eyes went glassy at my words and he gasped, his body jerking forward, his hips thrusting up. I felt his cock pulse and I gripped him harder. "My goodness, you are—"

But I didn't even have time to finish my sentence. Nathan cried out and tensed. He grabbed either side of my forearms like he was trying to thrust into me even though we were both fully clothed. "Oh god!" he said as his body spasmed.

And there it was. It was the

ring of lust and shame in the timbre of that cry when I knew. That's when I decided I just didn't give a fuck what anybody was going to say. I had to have him. I had to make him mine.

SATURDAY, FEBRUARY 4

I don't have to work until the afternoon today and it's a good thing. Since Nathan just left.

How do I describe what it's like for someone like me to be with someone like Nathan after spending what feels like a lifetime married to someone like HWSNBN? The momentous impact of what's just happened is only highlighted by the way my life used to be.

In retrospect I should have known things would not be good in bed with HWSNBN from the start. There are things I will always remember about that first time. The blue of the ocean out of the honeymoon suite window glimpsed from the bed over his shoulder. The faint smell of bleach the Caribbean cleaning staff used before each new guest. A few small cracks in the ceiling plaster. The intensity with which my normally jovial and easy going boyfriend of ten months and spouse of twelve hours said, "Okay, let's do this."

The other things, honestly, I don't try to recall. But they played like a damning loop in my head. A recording I've switched on every morning after that first time, one I couldn't seem to help but painstakingly add to with only the most searing words from each subsequent and progressively awkward coupling. In the end I had a highlight reel of the worst moments, a "greatest hits" from years of shame, a humiliation compilation.

I'd play my compilation. Not willingly, exactly. But out of a seemingly unstoppable, masochistic need to remind myself each day: This is who you are.

A woman whose husband finds her physically repulsive.

And then last night there was Nathan.

I know I wavered for a moment when he walked into the cottage and looked around, telling me that he and his buddy Owen are going to get their own place too, that he just can't live at home anymore. I admit, when my illicit thoughts clanged against the hard fact that this boy lives with his parents it was with a dissonance that made me cringe. Of course he lives with his parents. I faltered. But then in my mind's eye I saw limbs entangled. Bill's. Ashley's. Indignation and vengeance teamed with lust and I felt them make my body pulse with need. I closed my eyes.

"Take off my bra now," I told him steadily.

We were in bed semi-clothed. He managed the clasp of my bra well and I stopped myself from any patronizing comment, though a part of me wanted to. He pulled it away and looked at my naked torso. I felt almost stoned with power as his greedy eyes took me in. He put his hand up and cupped my left breast in his right hand and groaned. "Oh god," he whispered. He reached with his other hand too and moved to kiss me. There'd already been kissing, so much kissing, I forgot how much kissing there could be before sex becomes the foregone conclusion. But then his kisses got shaky and unfocussed. I could tell he just wanted to feel. I pulled back and lay on the bed. I took off my jeans so I was clad only in panties and his eyes burned trails all over me.

"Just touch me," I said. And he did.

He stared and stared like he couldn't get enough. Somewhere inside me it was like an arid, parched stretch of land where all the vegetation had withered from drought began to get rain. He moved his hands all over my exposed skin. His breathing got ragged.

"I want to give you pleasure," he said, using those words again that were my undoing. "I want you to show me how."

I reached over and took off his glasses, folded them and put them on my nightstand. "I'll show you my favorite way," I whispered and eased off my panties.

He looked down at me where I'd shaved myself almost completely, just left a little strip. His face flushed and he looked so adorably full of intent. He moved between my legs and I spread myself open for him with my hands, letting him see it all. I knew I was wet, wet from all the kissing and touching and anticipation. In my previous life I would have cringed in shame over this but somehow I didn't feel that at all with Nathan, just brash and brazen and wanting him to see. And he did. He looked mesmerized as he lay on his stomach and moved his face down close between my legs.

I know I shook slightly. It had been years since

anyone's mouth had been anywhere close to that sensitive part of me. I could have cried with the intensity of having him there.

"You smell so good," he breathed, looking up at me. "I'll just lick right here," he said and gave the tip of my clit a tiny, tentative lick. *Zing!* The pleasure of that one little caress of his tongue went all the way through me and I moaned, loud and long.

"Yes," I said. "Right there is good, sweetie. Very good."

He did it again then. More tentative little licks with his sweet tongue. "Mmm, yes, that's good," I said. "Nice and slow." I wanted to put my head back, close my eyes, but then I'd miss watching him and watching him was so good.

"Should I give it little kisses too?" he asked and I nodded because it was hard to speak. He kissed my clit and god did his full, red lips look good doing that. He got bolder then, kissing and licking, licking a bit faster, then slower, poking at me a bit with his tongue. I did put my head back then, closed my eyes, groaned in pleasure. His tongue was wild and had no rhythm to it at all and I didn't fucking care because I liked him using me to learn. After a while it was all I could do not to put my hand on the back of his head and command him to just lick hard and fast, as hard and fast as he could. But I didn't do that. Because his way was delicious in its hesitancy. Ten or fifteen years ago, before my marriage, I might have been frustrated, wanting the destination and not appreciating the journey. But this time with Nathan I wanted to savor every sensation. I lay back and gave myself over to him and his inexperienced little tongue.

"Does it feel better," he asked softly, "if I lick you lightly, like this … " and he peppered my burning nub with feather light little flicks that left me feeling floaty and gaspy. "Or harder ones, like this." And without further warning he jammed his tongue down on me ruthlessly, tonguing fast and hard while I screamed out. Then he stopped short with me dangling on the edge. He looked up at me, alarmed.

"Oh god, did I hurt you?"

"No," I rasped, panting and shaking. I felt my patience dwindling. "They're—they're both very nice, love," I said, when I could form words. "Let's do that second one again," I said, trying not to growl it at him. "But this time, if I start screaming, you just keep going." I felt fire in my eyes as I stared at him and saw realization dawn in his. "Okay?"

He lowered his head to do it again but just before he started he placed one then two soft kisses on my little bud all while looking straight up at me and the sweetness of that action combined with the exquisite feel of his lips pursed around my clit pierced into me. Then he went to work licking me hard and fast. And oh fuck, it did not take me long. I pushed my right hand through that floppy mess of his hair and held on tight, I couldn't help it, as I screamed and writhed on his face, forgetting everything I had been thinking about being gentle and patient. "Fucking christ!" I bawled out as his tongue worked me over the edge.

But then he kept going! Oh god, it was so sensitive and I tried to yell stop, to push him away but I couldn't make any sounds other than screams and he was still licking hard and intently, holding me by my thighs to his face, there was no stopping him and I guess I told him to keep going after all. Soon the sensitivity gave way to another orgasm. It was upon me before I realized it and it ripped through me faster than the first. All I could do was pant and gasp out, Oh god! Oh god! Oh my god!

Thankfully he stopped then. He looked up at me timidly and his face was so full of the need for approval I felt my heart break in two for how vulnerable he seemed at that moment.

"I wasn't sure when to stop," he said. "Was that good?"

I pulled him up to me. Gently I put his head to my breasts and stroked his hair, holding him on top of me. "It was so good, Nathan love. So good."

Oh! It's almost time to go to work. I am brimming with ideas for sketches.

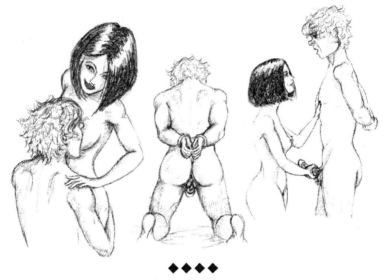

❖❖❖❖

It's odd. Nathan's 'Edward Harden' holds have been picked up. I wonder how he managed it without ID. He didn't mention he was coming to the library today. I would have thought he would take the opportunity to catch up on his sleep after last night! I guess that's the benefit of youth. Perhaps after the dynamic of our encounter he really wants to read more about power play.

And I don't know what the hell has crawled up Pig Face's butt today. When I got in at noon she gave me some big spiel about how the holds need to be wrapped, something about the title of the book not showing. When does she find the time to think up this bullshit? She really needs to get a life.

Monday, February 21

Delia called me five times yesterday. She knows the library was closed and I imagine she was picturing me holed up at the cottage by myself. I know I should have answered because I'm sure she's worried about me. I'm not even angry at her anymore and I shouldn't have been then. My anger at the restaurant was misplaced. But part of the reason I don't respond is because, while I have been holed up at the cottage, it hasn't been by myself. And if I talked to her I might tell her. I might tell her that Nathan came back again, that he's been here twice now. And if I tell her she will probably want me to stop. And I don't want to stop.

Here's another sorry truth from the history of my laughable marriage. When HWSNBN would finally acquiesce to my desperate cajoling and have sex with me, it was never a short encounter. Which sounds like a good thing. But trust me when I tell you it wasn't.

It didn't take a long time because we were embroiled in long slow kisses and intimate conversation, passionate foreplay leading to beautiful love making that ebbed and flowed, rolling like waves and ending in crashing orgasms. Not even close. Foreplay was a short series of awkward hugs and squeezes. Penetration was perfunctory. Then the actual sex went on. And on. And on.

I know a man who can last in the sack is supposed to be a good thing. Perhaps in other men it is. But with HWSNBN it was just ... boring. It was as though I wasn't even participating, like I was just flesh, just a vessel, just there. Whenever it seemed he might be getting close to an orgasm and I would attempt to stroke him or hold him or, god forbid, talk to him, he would grunt in apparent irritation, sigh, and have to start again.

Afterward, if I mentioned it he would be dismissive. "I just need to concentrate," was how he explained it. That's what I was to him during sex. A break in his concentration.

Ha, it's funny. Nathan needs to concentrate during sex with me too. But for an entirely different reason.

I just got off the phone with Dee.

I think there are people in your life who make things real. That is, if something's happened and I haven't talked to Dee about it, it's like it hasn't happened. This thing with Nathan, whatever's going on between us, I can't keep that from her. I need to talk about it. I tell Dee everything. Well, nearly everything. She was the first person I called the last time I was involved with someone losing his virginity. Of course that was HWSNBN. And it was my virginity too. And well … that was a different situation.

Anyway, I apologized to Dee for losing my cool at Gino's the other night. I told her that I know she's not going to be happy about what's going on with me but that I needed her to put that aside. That something big has happened. That I needed to talk to her about it.

And then I told her the story of how I, Charlotte Campbell, little library nerd, the same woman who mere months ago was really excited about spending her Saturday night installed on the couch next to her indifferent husband watching the latest episode of Downton Abbey that she'd PVRed, spent this past Saturday night initiating sweet, young Nathan into a world, not just of sex, not just of lust, but of submission. Submission to me.

I didn't mince words or shy away from the sordid facts of the situation: that this was indeed his first time and that he wanted his first time to be with someone older, someone experienced, someone like me. And I told Dee I wanted it. But perhaps I didn't say how much. Privately I know I was greedy for it. I wanted to orchestrate it, to conduct it for him, for me. I wanted it to be slow and savored. I wanted to see his face the first time he felt all the sensations that he's wondered about and tried to imagine for so long. I wanted all those first reactions, every gasp, every moan. I wanted them all. I wanted them for my own.

Yes, some things I kept to myself. How he begged, "Please Charlotte, please let me be inside you," and how his pleading was all the sweeter for the way his voice cracked in the middle. How his slim, pale body shook in anticipation as I grasped his cock and eased down his foreskin. God, how the sight of the shiny, purple head beneath made me long to suck him. But one thing in particular is just for me. He was sitting naked on my bed and I studied him as I straddled his boyish frame and placed his hardness against my slippery, wet entrance. His pupils were dilated and he looked like he was in a trance. When I slowly eased myself down on him, millimeter by millimeter, softly murmuring reminders for him to breathe, to relax, at the moment when I was pressed firmly down onto his lap enveloping him completely, I watched his shiny caramel eyes fill with tears. He smiled at me and those tears spilled onto his cheeks as he said, "Charlotte, you are so beautiful."

That moment I know will be my secret salvation for a long time to come. I will tuck that little morsel away in my mind, to take out and cherish in private moments.

I did tell Delia what happened next though. Once he was inside I almost involuntarily gripped him tight with my pussy muscles, I was so excited. He gasped and clutched at me. "Oh god, what is that? What are you doing?" he said, panicked, and the shaking in his body intensified. And then, without any movement, without one stroke or the slightest amount of rocking, I felt Nathan's fingers dig into my shoulder blades as his shaft stiffened in my depths. And he came.

When he came he cried out. And the sound of his

cry, the helplessness of it, well, it makes my pussy quiver and clench just thinking of it now. And if the sound of that helpless cry makes me wet, his words at that moment fill me with fire. Even as it was happening, he *apologized*. "Oh fuck, I'm sorry," he said. "God, I can't hold it!" he huffed through clenched teeth as his body jerked and spasmed inside of me.

As much as I need Delia to know the basics of what transpired between Nathan and me, I can't confess the most intrinsic part, the part that hits me at my core. How the idea of Nathan being weak in the face of my sexuality is an aphrodisiac so powerful to me I feel light-headed with the intoxication of it.

I didn't tell her what we did after Nathan lost his virginity. I didn't tell her that what I've been sketching since I met Nathan is unlike anything I've ever done before.

February 22

Fuck. Oh fuck.

When I came in this morning my head was full of what happened between Nathan and me on the weekend. I felt playful and sexy and, considering what we'd done, extremely powerful. So when I looked back at the "saucy little minx" comment he'd made in his last email, I was filled with playful, dominant indignation. I fired off a quick retort.

A comment like this would have earned you a spanking on Sunday.

Moments later, this was the reply.

Sunday? You must have me confused with someone else (how many library patrons do you communicate with this way?!) as I have been alone all week. And I'm certain a Sunday with you is something I would not soon forget.

My heart was beating in my throat, panic was rising in my belly, when this email came right after.

I'm glad to hear from you though. I'm sorry I missed meeting you when I came in on Saturday morning to pick up my holds. Jokes aside, I must admit that our communication has me intrigued and I confess that I even asked to speak to the person who processes the holds, hoping to meet you. In fact the woman who came out was someone named 'Sue' and I am ashamed to say I was relieved to find out her name was not Charlotte as she has a surprisingly porcine quality about her and an alarmingly aggressive demeanor. I made up some excuse about privacy in relation to the way the hold material is wrapped (some might find my area of interest risqué, after all!) so I hope I didn't get you into any trouble.

Anyway, if you can find time between your other spanking commitments (!) I wondered if you might like to meet for coffee? We could discuss the books I've checked out. Maybe the submissive one that you chose. Or if you prefer you could continue chastising me for requesting special favors or setting up a library account online and sending someone else to pick up my holds. Feel free to get in touch via text.

Best,
Ed Harden

WHAT??

If I haven't been emailing with Nathan all this time ... then who? Who the hell have I been flirting with about BDSM books??

◆◆◆◆

I just got off the phone with Nathan. I can't believe it.

Edward Harden is a real guy! It's not a fictitious account Nathan created for his holds. Edward is a work colleague of Nathan's dad who's in town on business this month. Nathan said his parents had him over for dinner the other night. Nathan was being pestered by his dad for "wasting library resources" and coming here to play online computer games. They got talking about classic books made into movies and Edward asked Nathan if he'd ever seen *To Kill a Mockingbird*. He said he hadn't. The next day Edward told him he'd put the movie on hold under his name and to pick it up the next time he was in.

Holy shit. What have I said? I'm trying to think back on what I wrote to Edward when I thought he was Nathan. Oh god. I *have* been chastising him! I put that submissive book on hold. I told him he had issues! But the worst part ... the worst part is that someone knows. Some man, some stranger, some random person out there is walking around knowing that there is this woman who works at the Parkdale Library ... who is into some kinky shit.

I don't normally listen to the messages HWSNBN leaves on my phone. I normally delete them on sight. I guess Delia's prodding is starting to get to me though. I didn't pick up when I saw his name come up today. But when my phone buzzed that a message had been left I started to listen.

> *Char? Honey? I don't know how many messages I've left now. I don't know if you're listening to these. But I really wish you'd call or even come by. We need to talk. It doesn't have to be like this. But we have to talk to each other. Look, I know I need to apologize to you. I know seeing what you saw must have been confusing and created a lot of questions about us. That's what I need to talk to you about, Char. This thing with Ashley, I did it for us! I know that sounds strange but things between us haven't been good for years. Isn't that what you were always telling me? That you needed more? Well I thought maybe we needed to, you know, mix things up. Not be so closed-minded. So anyway, Ashley and I, we think it would be a good idea for you to—*

That was when I deleted the message. I'm still shaking. He and Ashley. He and *Ashley*?? "We think it would be a good idea for you to—" We. He and Ashley are a "we" now. Trying to fathom a world were he and Ashley talk about things and make decisions together, I feel like my mind refuses to process it, like it's trying to multiply three digit numbers together, like it would hurt me deeply if only it made any bloody sense.

If only I could get out of this room. If only I had people to talk to. If only I had something other than this mindless task of moving books from one place to another then maybe my brain could stop dwelling on HWSNBN. Moments like these it feels like the cruelest torture to have been forced to work in the Dungeon at this point in my life. Here in the back with nothing to do but sit and stew and think and wonder and drive myself crazy. I wanted to puke my guts out, rip my head off, tear my heart out, anything to make myself stop thinking and hurting.

That was what I was thinking when Pig Face came back here and saw me being a bit rough with Fritz.

Charlotte what the hell are you doing? That's sensitive machinery you're slamming around!

After she left I actually patted Fritz. I actually uttered the words, "There, there, I didn't mean it."

Sigh.

I'm definitely calling Nathan tonight.

FEBRUARY 28

Nathan just knocked on the staff entrance door again. That boy is going to get me fired. I've never been so excited about something as mundane as potentially losing my shitty ass job.

God, the things he says to me.

I can't stop thinking of you. Your eyes, your skin, your smell. I'm hard all the time. I can't stop touching myself.

I drink in his words like they are water and I've just walked through the desert.

I smiled sweetly and told him to go away. But then I grabbed him, pressed my pelvis to his and whispered in his ear that he was a filthy, naughty boy and that we were going to have to do something about his dirty thoughts and his lack of control. I felt him rock hard against me and his moan was filled with greed and desperation. I pushed my hips forward and rubbed my mound against that hardness. "Don't you dare come without my permission, do you understand me?" I said. He nodded, wordless. I gave him a little shove. "Now get out of here."

It's amazing the way the sight of his snub nose, his cherry red lips, those eyes, so wide and innocent, fill me with such an intense desire to push him to his knees, to make him quiver with desperation, to make him obey my every command. I've always had my little **BDSM** fantasies but I didn't know how it would make me *feel*. Who knew these feelings were inside of me? Who knew I could be so power hungry?

When I think of how I took his sweet little cherry, how he came within seconds of being inside me, that slumbering beast that resides in my belly starts to uncoil and rise.

March 2

It's not bad, is it, that while I'm toying with Nathan I've continued to communicate with Edward?

I mean, I haven't seen him. I turned down his polite coffee invitation. He replied that he imagined I was taken and I thought, am I? By HWSNBN? *Ashley and I, we want to be together.* By Nathan? *Your eyes, your skin, your smell.*

I don't know what I am.

So Edward and I have been swapping some emails. Well, more than some. A lot.

I can't believe what I have admitted to him, this person I've never met. Since my guard was already down when I thought he was Nathan, I continued that way. I could hardly have said, "oh, before when I was being flirty I thought I was emailing your work colleague's son" and then pretended to be all professional. So the flirting continued. But then things, I don't know how to describe it, opened up? The discussions about the kinky stuff turned surprisingly cerebral.

Wow, he is so … interesting.

He is a font of information about all things BDSM. He says he reads a lot—online and in books, hence his holds—but I'm dying to know more about his practical experience. I sort of alluded to it, his real life experiences, which he calls "RL play," and he skirted around the 'who' of it. I get the feeling it's uncomfortable for him. About everything else though, he seems as open and eager to discuss things as I am. It is so refreshing to have someone to open up to this way! When I confessed to him in our most recent email exchange my interest in orgasm control he replied like this:

> I have to agree that almost all situations regarding orgasm control I find very exciting. I love to deny orgasm. I love forcing someone to orgasm when she is trying not to. I love forcing someone to orgasm repeatedly. I love making someone orgasm in different/difficult/ humiliating ways. All of that is so exciting.

When I read this my knees started to shake. As I sat

there staring at the monitor I could feel my pussy pulsing between my legs, my cleft moistening. I looked down and suddenly realized I was gripping the edge of the desk hard with my hand.

Exciting? Um, yes, I'd say so. To put it ... mildly.

What was I writing?

Oh, yes. These are the kinds of discussions I can have with Edward. I find I look forward to opening up my email, that I'm checking far more often.

I wonder what he looks like ... .

MARCH 6

Just reread my last entry. Speaking of forcing, I have found that I enjoy forcing Nathan to do things. And although he protests, his erect cock demonstrates that he really enjoys it.

Forced confessions are a good example of this. Yesterday was so much fun. I had him stand in front of me naked while I sat comfortably on the couch. When we're together I enjoy keeping him naked while I am clothed as it enforces the idea that I can have as much access to his body any time I want, whenever I need it, while he must wait in anticipation for what part of my body I might allow him to see, let alone touch. I had on my skinny jeans and a very low cut top. I fingered the edge of the neckline as I watched his eyes focus in on the tops of my breasts. The feeling of power in revealing a portion of yourself to someone and eliciting such a strong reaction is amazing. If I could bottle the look of lust on his face as he peered down into my cleavage I would. And then I would drink it for breakfast.

"I'm going to stroke you now," I said.

I stroked him as I had him tell me just how horny he'd been and how much he was dying for me to let him come. But then, after a few more questions, he confessed how much he perversely enjoys it when I deny him what he wants. Mmm, making him confess that was so delicious. His expression was so pained and yet filled with desire at the same time. I could see how conflicted he was. I cupped his balls and he moaned as I told him how full they felt. He was desperate for release and so making him tell me how much he enjoys the denial while he's experiencing that aching desperation is an exquisite torture. Inflicting it makes me wet.

But that wasn't the best and most interesting part. That came next.

He began thrusting his hips at me. I stopped my touches. "Nathan sweetie, keep still like a good boy. I'll set the pace. I know what's good for you," I said. "I can tell you're getting close. And you don't want to know what I'm going to do to you if you spill your mess all over my hand." His face demonstrates just how much he loves it when I talk about his orgasm that way.

"Oh, maybe I do," he said. His eyes were closed and it was though he was talking to himself.

"Is that so, little boy?" I asked.

"Yes," he murmured. "Oh Charlotte," he said, and I could tell from the way that conflicted look intensified that something really good was coming. "I want … ."

"What do you want, love?" I said, in a voice that was like syrup pouring from a jug.

"I want you to be mean to me."

Oh ho. The little boy with all of his romantic notions has had a change of heart it seems. Well I guess, so have I.

You see, I have spent my life being nice. Really, I enjoy being nice. One of the reasons I loved my job was that I enjoyed helping people find what they were looking for. And being nice. Smiling. Of course, that was before I got sent into the Dungeon where the only interaction I have is with Fritz. Now I smile at Fritz. He spits books at me.

Yes, I am a 'nice girl.' Or I was. But when Nathan made this confession I recognized that something in me has changed.

I want to be mean.

And when I want to be mean I can actually feel it change me. My eyes narrow. One side of my smile curves up. The beast uncoils. I become what Nathan now calls me:

Mistress.

March 8

Edward thinks they are wasting my talents, hiding me away in the Dungeon. No fucking kidding.

He asked me about what I liked about my work, back when my life was normal and I was allowed out with people.

What did I like about it? Well, it's not rocket science obviously, I wasn't saving lives, but I loved that job. I really felt it was the perfect job for me. I guess I wasted a lot of time in my twenties trying to figure out what I wanted to do. I tried a degree in fine arts but that didn't work out. I worked in advertising, in graphic design. That was soul destroying and the deadlines were toxic. I wanted to do something low stress but that I could feel passionate about, satisfied by. Then I started working for the library and I couldn't believe my luck. They paid me to talk to people about books, movies and music. They *paid* me for that. I felt like a little kid with a secret, like, shh, don't tell anyone but I would do this job for free.

Here's a little example to demonstrate what I loved about that job. One day a little girl came in looking for a princess book. She was about 8 or 9. While I was helping her find one she liked she mentioned to me that her mom was making her get this book but she "didn't like reading." I told her I was sure that wasn't the case, she just hadn't found the right books yet. I gave her the book *Ms. Brooks*

Loves Books (and I don't) about another little girl who thought she didn't like reading. I saw her connect with the character of the girl in the book. The next time that little girl came in, she searched me out. She wanted more. She actually wanted to read more. Now, I don't mean to sound too Pollyanna about it. Maybe that book did nothing for that little girl. But maybe it did. And if I am doing something on a regular basis to help promote reading, a love of literature, sharing ideas, expanding people's horizons, well. Then. My work here is done. Ha, ha. Okay, I don't really have that much of an inflated sense of myself. But I just like the idea that I'm putting out that kind of energy into the world, even in small, incremental ways.

Then Edward asked me about my BFA. I told him that I didn't complete it. Then I shared some more about my recent sad attempt at trying to do something serious with my artwork, how I started taking that class. I was vague about why I had to drop that too. God, he must think I'm such a flake, that I never finish anything I start. It seems like every time I start to move forward with my artwork something ... debilitating happens. I mean, I could hardly have continued on with my class this time. Not with *that person* there.

Anyway, he said he wants to see some of my work. And, I can't believe I did this but, I told him what I've been drawing.

Well, you see, um ... sometimes my artwork and my interest in BDSM collide.

Now he really wants to see.

MARCH 11

"Just use me, Charlotte. Use me," Nathan said. So I did.

God, I enjoy it. I so enjoy bossing him around, taking his horny desperation and toying with it, stoking it, building a fire in him. And using him.

When he was here yesterday he was even more desperate than usual. I hadn't seen him for a few days and I'd spent that time texting him, sending him photos of little portions of myself, the smooth skin beside my belly button, the paleness of the inside of my thigh. The slow doling out of these little snippets drove him wild. I gloried in his every response. "Charlotte! Your skin is so soft there. It feels like silk. Thinking of it makes my cock ache. Please let me come. I'm begging you." And of course the answer to that was no.

So yes, a crazy horny Nathan showed up on my doorstep yesterday. And when I opened the door I thought he might come in his pants right there.

I had done a little online shopping. I was deciding what I would wear when Nathan visited, flipping through little flirty dresses and cute tops, when I realized the woman who was dressing to play with Nathan was not going to find a thing in my closet. This was Mistress. And Mistress wanted black, wanted tight, wanted slutty and hard.

I pulled him inside and asked him if he was ready to be my little fuck slave. He could only nod. He looked stunned. His eyes traveled up and down my body, taking in everything from the dark makeup around my eyes and the bright red I'd painted my lips to the swell of my breasts pushing out of my corset, the tight leggings that accentuated the curves of my ass and the shiny black stiletto heels. I pushed him down onto his knees.

"Tell me what you're here for," I said.

"To serve you, Charlotte," Nathan said.

"You will call me Mistress when you are serving me," I told him.

He looked up at me quickly, his eyes alight with surprise. "Yes, Mistress! Oh I would love for you to be my Mistress."

"I know, little boy. Now strip."

He took off all his clothes. His cock was already hard and he put a protective hand in front of it, grasping it lightly as he stood naked in the middle of the living room looking shy and awkward. I felt power flowing into me as I watched him squirm.

"Did I say you could touch it?" I said, one eyebrow arched and looking at his hand on his member.

"Sorry, Mistress," he said, dropping his hand and

bowing his head

"Have you been practicing fucking like I told you to?"

"Yes," he whispered.

"What have you been using?"

He flinched. "You know, Mistress. You made me buy it."

I chuckled. "I know, boy. But I want to hear you say it."

His cheeks were aflame. "The stamina training unit."

"And what is that?" I asked, fixing him with an expectant stare. "Speak clearly now, so I can hear you."

He swallowed. "It's a fake pussy. It looks like a flashlight but it's a plastic pussy that I can ... use."

"Yes." I smiled sweetly. "It's appropriate for you, isn't it?"

"Yes, Mistress." If he hung his head any lower it looked like it would fall off his shoulders.

"Is it working?" I asked him.

"Oh, Charlotte. I mean, Mistress. No, it's not. But you don't let me come in it! It just makes me more desperate for your beautiful pussy. It's so humiliating having to, you know, put myself in that one."

"And tell me what that humiliation does to you," I said.

He got quiet again. "It makes me so hard," he whispered.

I made him follow me into the bedroom on his knees. Once there I put my hand on the back of his head and pushed his nose between my legs. "That's what you want, isn't it?" I said as I listened to him breathe me in.

"Fuck, you smell so good. Yes, Mistress. Please!"

"But you are here to serve me, remember? So are you going to be a good boy and lie down and be my fuck stick now? You have two rules: Stay hard. Don't come."

I so enjoyed the look of panic on his face. I ordered him onto the bed, on his back. His cock was rigid over his pelvis. I remembered how he begged for mean and so I knelt beside him and gave that hard flesh two quick slaps. He gasped and his hands flew instinctively to cover himself.

"Hands off," I said, steel in my voice. "Your cock is mine. I can do what I like with it. I could tell you were too excited and you were never going to last in my pussy. I was helping you." I looked deep in his eyes. "Now put your hands down by your sides. And keep them there."

The anticipation of Nathan's visit had me wet before he even stepped in the door. Now that he was on my bed, naked and prepared for anything I wanted to do to him, my pussy was spasming with need. I peeled off my pants and watched his face as I revealed my bare pussy. I put my fingers inside myself, coated them with my wetness and then smeared it on his face, marking what was mine. I straddled his lanky frame and took his cock in my hand.

"Remember. Stay hard. Don't come."

"Oh god, Charlotte, Mistress, I don't think I can—"

But I put my hand over his mouth as I sank myself down on him. His eyes widened and I felt his whole body tense. I locked his hands down by his sides with my legs. "Shut the fuck up," I said, watching his eyes get even wider.

He whimpered into my hand as I rode him. I kept my hand over his mouth, the feeling of overpowering him and taking him fueling my thrusts. After only a minute he started shaking his head and saying something into my hand.

"I told you to shut up while I fuck you, slave," I whispered into his ear, thrusting harder on him. I felt him go rigid inside me. Then he was crying out behind my hand as his body convulsed.

Watching Nathan's pallor of shame as I made him admit what he'd done fed the beast in me that was Mistress. "Now go down and clean up your mess. Make me come with your tongue since you couldn't do it with your cock," I said as I lay back and he moved over me. I put my hand on top of his head and pushed him down for the second time that day.

I've had that image, my hand on his head, in my mind ever since. It's burned there, like a symbol of the status of our relationship.

MARCH 15

I called Dee today to ask if she remembered that my dad used to make us stay behind to scrub the pews in church when we were bad.

"When we were bad?"

"Yeah, when we were talking during his sermon. Do you remember?"

She said she thought she remembered that vaguely and why was I asking. So I told her about the dreams.

"Huh," she said.

"What do you think it means?" I asked her.

"That you have Daddy issues," Dee said. "Obviously. Or cleaning. You have cleaning issues."

I looked around the cluttered cottage. "Dee, I'm serious. It's more like a nightmare. It scares me," I told her.

She asked me what about it was scary but I couldn't explain it. I know it doesn't sound like a scary dream. But it is.

For me, it is.

MARCH 16

Edward is flying back home in five days. I really want to meet him before he goes off again.

I finally relented and sent him one of my sketches. It was thrilling and terrifying to share. Even just scanning it onto the USB stick to email it made my heart race. I sent the one of me and Nathan in the alley. After I sent it I checked my email about every thirty seconds to see if he'd responded. I was so focused on what he would think of me in the sketch and of my sketching generally that I forgot all about the other person in the sketch. And damn if he didn't recognize Nathan.

Here is the thing about Edward. I want to tell him things. Things that are deep inside of me. Even though we've still never met, after all our sharing via email there's one thing I know. He gets me. So even though I was initially horrified when he recognized Nathan, I eventually confessed that it was not just a fantasy, that I was exploring dominance with him. I don't know what I expected. I think some part of me was waiting for judgment, for someone to tell me I was wrong and bad. But he wrote:

> He seems like a good kid. I would have loved some attention like that when I was his age. Especially from someone as sexy as you.

When I read that I could feel a huge grin spread across my face. And then I read the next part.

> I know it was hard for you to share your work. I know you're embarrassed by it and you keep it hidden. I just want you to know I'm honored to be the first to see. Charlotte, your sketching is brilliant. It's inspired. You're very talented. And I'm proud of you for finding the courage to show me.

He said he was proud of me. Proud.

It's so hard to describe how that makes me feel. For so long now my drawings have been a source of shame.

I'm compelled to create them and yet when I'm done I feel equally compelled to hide them.

That shame. Buried so deep down.

Then there was Edward, not only accepting what I've drawn but saying he was proud of me for showing them. *I'm proud of you.* Did he know how badly I needed those words? I felt them tapping into a deep wound. Soothing it. But there was another feeling. I'd been carrying that around with me all day, the other feeling. For some reason it made me feel ... hot? Something. A funny little feeling in the pit of my stomach.

Why am I feeling this way about someone I've never met? Especially with everything going on with Nathan. I mean, I adore Nathan. He's such a sweetheart. And yet I feel something pulling me towards Edward.

He asked me again to meet him. Before he leaves. Really, what is the point in that?

But I want to.

Because there's one other exchange we had. Something I can't stop thinking about.

I was telling him about the mixed feelings of the desire to dominate and subjugate but also to care for and nurture that I feel with Nathan. And I wondered what it would be like to have someone feel that for me.

Well, many in the BDSM community feel that a proper dominant should experience submission so that she understands both sides of the coin. So perhaps that is a relationship you should seek out. :)

With a little smiley on the end like that! Does he mean him? Is he suggesting that I should seek out a relationship like that with him?

MARCH 18

At Gino's tonight, over panzerottis as usual, I asked Dee if she thinks I should meet Edward.

"So you've been emailing with him for about a month?" she asked.

"Right."

"And you've never met him."

"That's right," I said.

"Because of Nathan?" she asked.

"Pretty much, yes."

"But now you want to meet him anyway. Why?"

"I don't know. We just have these great conversations. There's something about him. He's wise and charming and so ... sexy. But he's leaving in two days. It's silly, right?"

Dee didn't say it was silly, though. "He could be ugly. Or fat. What if he's really fat? Then would he still be charming and sexy?"

"Delia!" She was smiling, chomping on her fries. "Just tell me if you think I'm crazy for wanting to meet some guy who doesn't even live in the same city when I am having a great time with Nathan."

"Who's half your age," she quickly shot at me. When is Dee going to get past the age thing? "Do you know how old Edward is?"

"He's 47."

"Wow, you're really going for the opposite ends of the spectrum."

"Just tell me what I should do!"

She ended up saying I might as well. What could it hurt? Otherwise I'll always wonder. Then she asked about HWSNBN.

"Fuck him," I said.

"So still not ready to talk about it?" she asked wryly.

I don't know what the fuck she thinks there is for me to talk about.

MARCH 19

It's late and I'm so tired but I have to write down what happened today. I met Edward. And now I don't know what to do with myself.

I told him I would meet him tomorrow. We made plans to have a drink in the hotel bar where he's staying. All day with Fritz I couldn't stop thinking about it. About meeting him. What would he look like? What would we talk about? Would it be as easy as it seemed via email? Or would it be awkward?

There I was, lost in thought as I scanned books through and printed hold slips, so I didn't even notice what book it was that I plucked out of Fritz's hold bin until the slip popped out.

HARDEN, EDWARD. *On Being a Good Submissive*

I jumped. The hold I placed for him! Should I check it out and bring it tomorrow, I wondered. It seemed strangely presumptuous. But he was leaving. He wouldn't be able to take it anyway.

An hour later I was shelving the holds out in the library when I felt someone behind me. It's so amazing but I remember the feeling of him standing there. How I knew before I turned, before he even spoke and said his name, that it was him. I could *feel* him. I turned ... and saw Edward for the first time.

I'm looking for my hold. The last name is Harden.

I looked back at the shelf to find his name and get his book. I was breathing hard. I tried to recover myself, tried to talk and fill up the space between us that seemed so charged with some strange tension I'd never felt. I handed it to him. His eyes. They held mine and seemed to speak volumes even when he was silent in that moment. I turned away and made some rambling comment about the plain cover of the book he was checking out being so different from the racy contents within. What he said next wasn't anything explicitly sexual. But there was a heat in it that made my knees weak and my head woozy.

He said, "I do like things that look one way on the outside but when you open them up, reveal themselves to be quite different on the inside." I swallowed hard. Again, I could feel him behind me eying me with such intensity. "I know people like that," he said, stepping up close to my back, the physicality of him so near, his breath at my neck as I stood staring at all those names on the hold shelf while this man I'd never met whispered, "like one innocent looking girl who works in the library."

My heart was slamming in my chest. He cleared his throat. I turned around to face him and he handed the book back to me. "Now that I see this I realize I don't need it after all." He smiled. "But maybe you'd like to read it." I looked down at the cover. *On Being a Good Submissive.* My face flushed, I was simply unable to speak. "I'll see you tomorrow," he whispered.

Then he was gone.

March 22

Nathan knows something is up.

I haven't seen him since I met Edward in the library. We've been texting but it's not our usual sexy texts. He's asked me a couple of times what's wrong but I told him I'm fine. I don't know what else to say to him.

I should just keep my mouth shut about what happened with Edward. He's gone now, he flew out yesterday, so that's that. Except, if I'm honest with myself, I don't want that to be that. That cannot be that. Even if I can't see him. Even if it's just via email. I crave his words.

I crave the way he makes me feel. Especially after what happened when I met him at his hotel.

Oh god, what happened. If I shut my eyes I can still feel his hands on me. Images of it repeatedly flash through my head. I've been wet constantly ever since. Every time I cross my legs I have a small, quick orgasmic spasm.

It was clear the moment I walked into the bar and our eyes met that the dynamic between us was not going to be one of friendly, flirty banter, the way it had been with our emails. It was different now. Something about when we met at the library had changed things. The way he looked at me, the way he raised his eyebrow as I walked toward him, his calm, sexy smile triggered something inside me. I could feel it, not in the way that I felt Mistress, when she rose up and took over. Mistress came and went. This was something that always resided in me, that felt a part of my core.

It was as though he could see into my thoughts because he said, "I think it's cute how you are playing at being a Domme to that boy." And while I stammered, trying to come up with a reply, he added, "When it's obvious to me what your true nature is."

His eyes seemed all-knowing and his gaze made me squirm. My true nature. How did he know? Was there something about me that gave away the fantasies I always had? I wanted to ask but Edward was in control. He pulled confessions out of me, one after the other as we sat in the quiet bar. It was terrifying and thrilling and after each one I only wanted to give him more. How I longed to be controlled, to be owned, to be used, to be ... his. It was as though he'd tapped into a chamber of lava that was bubbling deep inside me that, once accessed, forced all my secret desires to spill forth and flow out.

"What is your ultimate fantasy?" he said, his voice low. "What is the one thing that gets conjured up in that pretty little head of yours over and over again?

"How do you know there is one thing?" I said, blushing so deeply it seemed like I could feel it in the roots of my hair.

"Oh, I know," he said with a smugness so sexy it practically took my breath away. Since when was smugness sexy? Since Edward.

I swallowed and didn't speak for a moment.

"Little girl," he said, and I gasped—at the sudden endearment and how it made me feel so small, so submissive, as I curled my fist at my mouth. "I know there is one, that fantasy that you've visited so often in your mind, your 'go to' thought that's like an especially skilled old lover: It gets you there every time." He took a sip of his drink. "It's written all over you." He paused. "What's more," he said, "I know you want to tell me. So go on, now. Tell me."

I kept my gaze on the small round table in front of us and fingered the stem of my wine glass as I spoke in a soft, tiny voice. "You strip me," I said, forcing the words out. "You tie me to the bed with my knees up and my pussy open to you." I pressed my eyes shut tight as I said the word "pussy" but continued on. "You tell me you want to lick me. Lick me all over but mostly between my legs. You tell me you enjoy the taste, the smell, the feel of that smooth skin on your tongue. It's enjoyable for you. And …" I suddenly realized I needed air and gasped in a breath. "And you want to do it for a long time," I said, my voice just a raspy, thin whisper then. "You want to do it for hours and you don't want me to come. I need to hold my orgasm in for as long as you say because you feel like eating pussy and you don't want to stop for some little slut who can't hold her come."

I kept my eyes down, staring at the table for what felt like an eternity, waiting for him to say something, anything. When no words came I finally managed to look up. He was staring at me. His eyes were dark. His mouth was almost in a grimace. If I didn't know better I'd have thought what I said had made him very angry.

"Your fantasy is very … compelling," he said, and his voice was growly and dangerous. He looked like some jungle animal, one of the big, stealthy cats ready to pounce on its prey at any moment. I could see his chest rise and fall. "Charlotte," he said, "You need to tell me now, what do you want?" We stared at each other and there was that electrical charge in the space between us again. "Do you want to submit to me? Do you want to experience what it's like?" He bowed his head a moment and then looked back up. "Just for tonight?"

I did. I wanted it so badly. All of my confessions

had me wet and aching. I felt needy and open. When he put his hand across the table and touched mine, our bodies connecting for the first time, I felt the shock of it course all through me. It made me want to kneel at his feet. "Yes," I gasped. "Please."

I went with him to his room. I was shaking with need. With fear. I only wanted to be good enough, to please him, this man who seemed to be able to see into my soul. "You will address me as Sir." I nodded with enthusiasm. "And you will do as I say."

"Yes, Sir."

I stood in the middle of his hotel room as he circled me. "For tonight, my pretty little pet, I own you." He looked deep into my eyes. "And I want to see what is mine."

I followed his instructions as he had me undress slowly, inspecting every part of me. It was mortifying to reveal my body so gradually to him this way, with him fully dressed and at his word, so I could barely understand why my pussy was soaked with wanting.

I was down to my panties and bra. He motioned for me to remove those too and I know he saw the look of uncertainty in my eyes. Somehow it was easy as Mistress to strip for Nathan but now, as Sir's "pretty little pet" I was a bundle of nerves. What if he didn't like what he saw? But he'd instructed me to strip. I looked in his eyes and saw patience, gentleness and also a dark hunger. It spurred me on. I unhooked the clasp of my bra at the back and cupped my hands to the front, easing it off, timidly exposing my breasts to him. Then I eased my panties down and kicked them away. Up until now he'd kept his calm, cool demeanor. But as he gazed at the smooth white rounded flesh of my breasts and rosy pink nipples and then down to the soft curled tendrils of hair between my legs, his eyes went soft. For a moment all of his sexy dominance was gone and his gaze was naked, not a lustful stare this time, but full of awe and appreciation. "You are so beautiful," he whispered as he reached his hand out to touch me. He cupped my breasts in his hands, gently teasing the tips with his fingers, then knelt on one knee to take a nipple in his mouth. He grazed it with his teeth, then sucked and licked it before giving the same attention to the other one. Then, still cupping them, he leaned his head forward and placed it between my breasts, just breathing there a moment. I put my hand on his head and held him.

When he rose from the floor to his full height and looked down at me, the cool dominance was back. "Your body pleases me greatly, my pet," he said.

He called me pet and that's how I felt, like his little puppy eager to please him. He continued touching me, circling around me with a keen eye, teasing and caressing my body until I was mad with desire.

I begged for things. I begged him to let me touch him, to let me see his cock. When he finally revealed himself to me, I sank to my knees. He was so big. The size of him made me feel even smaller and ever more desperate to serve him. When I took him in my mouth and looked up at him he grabbed a handful of my hair and said, "Good girl. Suck me like the little slut we both know you are."

Oh god, fucking him was like nothing I'd ever experienced before. By the time he eased his cock inside me, I was so wet and worked up I felt my orgasm start to build at the first connection of the base of him with my clit. I was stretched and full of him and all I could think of was how badly I wanted him to thrust and thrust. But he knew what I really wanted. What that place inside me needed. He pushed his enormous hardness into me and just as I began to match his thrusts, pushing my hips up at him, seeking the pressure on my clit that would drive me over, he held me and stopped. "Who's in charge of your little pussy tonight?" he growled. God, thinking of how he said that makes me cream even now. He drove me to the brink and backed off so many times I thought I was going to die. I begged him, begged him with everything I had to please, please let me come. And when he finally did, when he thrust into me and didn't stop, he held my head between his hands and forced me to keep looking at him as my body crested. "Look at me, little girl, and remember that I say when you can come. You may do it now."

And I came. I came like a raging river crashing down over a cliff, like claps of thunder cracking in the sky. I came at his word. I came harder than I ever have in my life.

March 30

Edward and I email each other everyday now that he's home. I created an email account just for our communication, so I could keep all his words to me in one place. I look forward to opening it with a compulsive intensity. I check it constantly. When there is something from him the joy and anticipation that wells up in me is exhilarating. I'm like a junkie getting a hit.

Sometimes it scares me.

I thought maybe I could see him again. I imagined that his visit here was perhaps a routine thing. But when I asked him how often he's here he said he rarely travels for work, that this was a special circumstance, there was a publishing conference he had to attend. He said it's difficult for him to get away.

I'm not sure what he meant by that.

APRIL 1

CURTIS, NATHAN P. *Tree Planting: A Survival Guide*

Nathan told me a few weeks ago that he was going to go tree planting for the beginning of the summer with his friend Owen as soon as his exams were over. It's the second year he's spent the summer making the money he needs for school by planting trees. When his hold came in for him today I remembered that he'll be gone in a week.

I haven't deliberately been keeping my relationship with Edward from Nathan. He just wouldn't understand. And anyway, Edward and I aren't actually having sex, not apart from that first time. So there's really no point in telling him.

Last night when Nathan came to the cottage he was quiet. "Mistress, I don't know how I'll survive the time

without you," he said with such sadness in his eyes. I wanted to take him in my arms and comfort him. So I did ... but we ended up in this position.

APRIL 10

When I opened my email from Sir today a page came up that displayed five beautiful pieces of jewelry: a necklace, a toe ring, an anklet, a bracelet and a ring. With it was this note:

My dearest little pet,

This is your first task. I would like you to look at these five items of jewelry and tell me which one of the five you feel the most drawn to. Is there one that speaks to you? That stirs a feeling inside? That's what I want to know. I would like your answer by 5 p.m. today.

Sir

Wow. What is he doing? What am I doing? What does this mean?

My brain is spinning with questions. But mostly, above all, the most overriding feeling is excitement. I am excited to be completing this first task for Sir.

But oh, I'm dying to know, what is it for? Am I going to get one of these? What am I going to do with it? Why does it fill me with submissive fervor to not know, to have him keep me in suspense? I can't explain it but to be following his instructions and picking out a piece of jewelry without question, simply because he told me to, lights me up inside.

I gazed at the items. They were all silver pieces that gleamed from a black background. The necklace was a simple but elegant chain with a pendant that was two circles linked together. The toe ring was sweet, a thin band with little curly cues that went out in opposite directions. The anklet was a fine chain with a tiny heart dangling from it that had a pink stone inset. The bracelet was the chunkiest item, a thick rope with different pink glass beads all around. I adored that one. That one was almost my favorite.

But the ring. The band was a brushed silver that worked into an intricate filigree pattern in the front. The filigree surrounded an onyx and white yin yang symbol in the centre. And Sir was right when he suggested that one might stir a feeling. I felt a little tingle in the pit of my stomach when I saw it.

Melody poked her head in to the Dungeon and saw me gazing at the items. "Ooh, those are gorgeous!" she said.

"They really are, aren't they?" I said.

"What are they for?" she asked.

"I … I don't know," I said, grinning like a mad woman.

"Well, where did they come from?" she asked, staring at me.

"Um, I'm not really sure," I said, looking to the side. She blinked at me.

"Charlie, are you feeling okay?" she said. "You look flushed."

"Yeah, I'm fine," I said, the mad grin back. "I'm really great," I said, as I thought about that ring on my finger, and of Sir and of how it felt to have his hand on mine, to have him hold my hair tight as he touched me wherever he liked.

April 12

When I told Sir that I keep a diary he said that he would sometimes like to direct what I sketch and write. He says I need to write about the things that embarrass me for his amusement. It's such a strange allure, to enjoy how he embarrasses me. Part of me wants to run screaming while another part wants to beg for more.

On Skype the other day we had a long chat. Today he said he wants me to write about what we discussed. So I will of course comply, even though some of it is difficult. My cheeks feel hot already just thinking about writing it. But I'm starting to realize how doing difficult things for Sir fills my little submissive heart.

He wanted to know about my marriage. I told him that Bill and I rarely had sex. Then he asked me about masturbation. I cringed but confessed that I would masturbate daily, sometimes having to come as many as four times in a row before I felt sated. Having to look into his eyes while I said these things was sweet torture. I could see how it surprised him but also turned him on to know what a horny little slut I always am. I told him I used to I fantasize about a strict Dom who would take control of my orgasms. I thought I wanted someone who was stern and would force me to submit to him.

But then he came into my life, Edward, Sir. I think it's wonderful that we ever met, we two who have so much in common, so many kinks that match up. And he introduced me to sensual domination. The Dom in my head was always stern and cold. Sir is firm and strict, but also loving, affectionate and playful. He does not force me to submit. I submit to him because serving and pleasing him fulfils me in a way I've never experienced before. His control of me makes my heart race and my knees literally feel weak. Sometimes he will simply raise an eyebrow and I feel like I could faint for how it fills me with a potent mix of lust, submissiveness and adoration.

My body and my orgasms are no longer mine. They are Sir's. I know now the daily masturbation and frequent multiple orgasms I used to give myself are because I'm a naughty, slutty, greedy little girl who cannot control herself.

So now he controls me. The last time he let me come was when we were together in his hotel room but it feels like much longer ago. I am desperate, desperate to release. But I may not. I get close. I edge for him. Lots of edges. Edges over and over. But I hold my orgasm, my "little cummie" as he calls it, until he says I may give it to him.

April 15

I love today! Today is an amazingly wonderful day!

They let me out of the Dungeon! I guess Pig Face has decided I've been punished enough for my little, shall we say, indiscretion, and that I can be allowed back on the floor to interact with the public. Too bad nobody can limit Pig Face's interactions with the public. I'm sure Nathan was significantly less traumatized by what occurred between us than say, lovely old Mr. Pickles (who tells everyone who'll listen that he will be on the local cable network news channel next month when he celebrates his 100th birthday) when Piggie barked at him for chatting too long with Melody at the check out desk. But I digress.

Yes, I found out today that yesterday was my last shift with Fritz. As if in protest, Fritz had one of his tantrums and shut down, refusing to check in anymore material. Mel put up the Out of Order sign and, even though I just got my Get Out of Jail Free card, I went back to help check in the books and I didn't even grumble about having to do it. Mel came back too and commented that I was awfully quiet. I couldn't help it. I was lost in thought about the other wonderful thing that happened today.

I got a package. As soon as I saw it my heart kicked up a fuss and when I saw Sir's name in the return address space I thought I might have a heart attack. I tore the padded envelope and withdrew a small box. It had a white lid, a black base and a black ribbon attached to the base that was tied over the lid in a bow, holding it in place. With shaking hands I tugged at one strand of the ribbon and it fell away. Slowly I lifted the lid. Inside there was black foam with a circular cutout that held a small round metal container. I pulled out the metal container, opened its lid as well, and there, settled on a puff of white batting, was the ring I had chosen.

I gasped. It was even more striking in real life than the photo I saw. The black onyx of the yin side gave off a dark sheen and the white yang side glowed. The filigree surrounding it was fine and beautiful.

I picked it up and held it gently between my thumb and forefinger. That's when I spied the inscription and tears sprung to my eyes.

For Pet. Your Sir.

My Sir, I thought. I was his. But he was also mine.

I noticed a slip of paper still inside the envelope. A note from Sir. In it he explained that my new ring would be a symbol of my submission to him. I was to place it on my hand for the first time after performing a special ritual during which I would strip naked, kneel sitting back on my heels with my legs parted in a slight V, and sit there holding the ring for five minutes while I thought about why I am choosing to pledge myself to him in this way. Then I was to put the ring on, kiss it and say, "My pleasure is to give Sir pleasure." After this ritual was performed I was not to take the ring off until such time as we agreed that my submission would end. Whenever I saw the ring on my hand, Sir wrote, it would act as a reminder to me that I do not have control over my body and my orgasms. They belonged to Sir.

My Sir.

I have now completed the ritual and I cannot wait to talk to Sir, to tell him how I enjoyed pledging my body to him in this way. He says we can Skype tomorrow … .

APRIL 17

I am back!

Today was my first day back at the customer service desk at work. On Skype the night before, Sir helped me choose what I would wear. He said it gives him pleasure to dress his little girl and it is certainly so much fun for me to try on different outfits I hope he will like. In the end he chose a black pencil skirt and white blouse, very conservative and suitable for the library. But then he chose the sluttiest bra and g-string panties I own to wear underneath. Oh god! At first I argued, saying that someone might see the black lace of the quarter cup bra beneath my white shirt. Or what if my bare nipples became hard and visible beneath my blouse! Not to mention how wearing the g-string under a skirt would leave me feeling naked and exposed. He just chuckled. "You'll be fine, pet," he said and reminded me how he enjoys the juxtaposition of the conservative outward look with the secret sluttiness underneath.

All day I was wet with my secret, that I am Sir's, that I belong to him, that I was wearing what he instructed. Wet and bright and alive. All the cheeriness and joy I used to have before I got sent to the Dungeon came flooding back. I flitted from one person to the next, searching, helping, loving being of service to people. It seems submitting to Sir fuels my desire to serve generally.

APRIL 22

I told Sir about Nathan wanting me to be mean and how sometimes I struggled to understand his desire for that. He asked me about when I wore the slutty g-string panties and bra for him, did I think that was a bit mean? And a light went on in my head. It did seem a bit mean, but in an evil and fun sort of way. I enjoyed him forcing me. I strangely enjoyed the potential embarrassment.

So Sir asked me to draw a sketch of what happened

when we Skyped the other night. Again the lure of erotic humiliation is a strange, strange beast indeed. I really don't want to … and yet a part of me has a twisted need to recreate it. It is a need I would never sate, for it would be far outweighed by embarrassment were it not for Sir. But Sir has instructed me to do it. And so I will.

I'm afraid next he'll make me write about it.

APRIL 25

Dee asked me at our dinner tonight if I miss Nathan. I told her I do. He doesn't have any Wi-Fi access out where he is so our communication is actually old school. He actually sends me sweet little letters of how he misses me and dreams of me at night, of holding me and kissing me gently.

Of course he's sent some not so sweet ones as well.

Since he was going to be gone for so long I removed his restrictions on coming. I couldn't be that mean. So he's been furiously jacking it at night like the horny boy he is. But he tells me how he longs to have me restrict him again.

He's desperate for punishment. He wrote that he cannot stop thinking about when I slapped his cock, how it stung and surprised him but also turned him on, drove him down further into his submission. He told me the most frustrating but intense orgasm he's had while he's been there on his own was when he fantasized I was teasing him about his lack of stamina and he came while he was slapping his cock as I had done, trying to hold it back.

"And what about your sketching," Dee asked, propelling me out of my sweet, dark thoughts of Nathan.

I was glad she asked. I needed to talk to her about what Sir has suggested. But I needed a little push to do it.

My face felt so hot and I stumbled over my words as I explained to her that Sir thinks the graphic arts department at Xander Publishing where he works might be interested in my sketches. I have never really talked to Delia about the 'other' sketches I do. I've certainly never shown her one. I didn't know how she'd react. But when I was done explaining she looked excited.

"Can I see one?" she said.

My hands trembled as I reached for my phone where I'd saved digital copies of my sketches. Aside from Sir, any time anyone has seen this kind of sketch of mine in the past, all hell has broken lose.

I reminded Delia again that what she was about to see was graphic. Then I closed my eyes, put my head down and handed her the phone with the image of me and Nathan in the alleyway displayed.

"He's totally right," Dee said after what felt like an eternity of her staring silently at the screen. "You should submit this. Char, this is the best work of yours I've ever seen."

I sat for a moment, taking in the fact that Dee, whose work and opinion I admire so much, thought my sketch was that good. When I protested about the content she scoffed. "This has commercial viability, Char. You work in the library, you know what's in those graphic novels. And Edward's in publishing? It's perfect."

But what about before, I wanted to ask her. What about the fact that these pictures I draw always bring misery?

APRIL 30

One of the things I can enjoy now that I don't spend all day in the Dungeon is using nail polish again. Working with Fritz, taking things in and out of his bins, lifting crates and moving carts routinely caused my fingernails to chip and break so there was no point in keeping them pretty. I clipped them short. That, along with the boring jeans and t-shirts and clumpy big shoes I had to wear for practicality and safety, just added to everything I hated about being back there.

But no more. Today I've painted my nails a pretty light pink. Sir has decided that pink is the color that symbolizes my submission to him. Whenever I looked at my hands today, as I typed into the computer, searching databases or entering card information, both my ring and my fingernails announced to me that I am his.

MAY 2

I love to share everything from my diary with Sir. I love when he directs what I write or draw about. Today he wants me to write about the last drawing I did for him, the pigtails and the pillow. I'm taking a deep breath ... and doing it.

I confessed a secret to Sir. A secret about how I masturbate. It was very difficult to confess. I was horribly embarrassed. But again, this weird thing. I wanted him to know.

I explained that my most frequently used method of masturbation was to ... um ... put a pillow between my legs. I press myself in my panties, against the edge of the pillow and thrust myself against it until I come. Sir finds it very amusing how, using this method, I can generally come in under two minutes, sometimes less, and most certainly less if Sir is teasing me and then allows me to come.

Sir says it's such a horny little girl thing to do, to masturbate with a pillow. His next email to me was this:

My dearest pet,

What an interesting confession you had for me tonight! It is delightful to hear the creative ways you find to bring pleasure to your greedy little body. I can just imagine what a horny, slutty girl you look like, humping away on your pillow. But pet, do I really need to imagine it?
That's right, little girl. I would like to see.
Aw, I can just imagine how you are squealing and cringing

right now thinking about showing me. That's adorable. But you know how you love to please me and give me what I want. And you know deep down that you really want to. Don't you, pet?

The next time we play on Skype I would like you to prepare yourself in the following ways:

1) wear those cute little pink jammies I sent you

2) put your hair in pigtails

3) make sure your pillow is close by

Sir

Of course he was right. I did squeal and cringe and cover my face with my hands even though I was all alone. I could never have imagined someone witnessing such a private and embarrassing act. When I read what he wanted I immediately thought there was no way I could do that. Simply no way.

But of course he was also right about wanting to. It was a chant in my heart that went along with its beating: *make me, make me, make me.*

If the thought of being in pigtails and furiously humping my pillow crushed me with embarrassment, I hadn't realized that actually doing it was even more embarrassing than I'd pictured it. There were things I hadn't considered, like the fact that Sir could see my hair swinging in its pigtails as I was moving. Oh! It made me feel so shy, so … little. It would have been completely, cripplingly mortifying were it not for one thing: To give up my power and give it over to Sir is like a drug. The helpless feeling flipped that shame into the most erotic heat.

Sir also said I should include that in the past, before Sir controlled me, I would use this method to come quickly. So now, it is very difficult for me to stop at the critical moment when I pleasure myself this way. He noted my struggle with amused patience.

It is a new control my little body must get used to, he said.

Sir said he'd make sure I get lots of practice.

MAY 18

My pleasure is to give Sir pleasure. I've realized the deep sense of satisfaction I get from pleasing him. Sir explained tonight that often what pleases him is for me to be denied. But not always. Sometimes he said, he finds it amusing for me to come.

But not come like a regular girl. A regular girl would come once or twice during sex with her partner. But I am Sir's horny little slut. So sometimes he said he will demand what he calls a cum-slut training session.

A cum-slut training session, he explained, is when he gives me instructions about edging … and coming. Coming over and over and over again. Coming with my fingers. Coming with my vibrator. Coming with the pillow. A lot of that. "I want you coming until that little pussy is sore and you can barely ring another spasm out of your little, horny, over-stimulated body," he said.

He has denied me an orgasm for so long now. I can tell he is loving to tease me with the possibility of a cum slut training session. And like a starving person dreams of gorging herself on food, I am fantasizing of coming my little brains out at Sir's direction. He dangles these sessions before my denied, come-starved brain and body, using words like "intensive", "demanding" and "rigorous" … words that make me cream into my little panties with desire.

Sir has mentioned cum slut training a few times, but nothing yet that would suggest a session is imminent.

I can only live in hope.

May 20

Today Sir has said I should write about the different ways he allows me to have a cummie.

I've written about the pillow. Sir has allowed me to press myself against the pillow and "wiggle out my relief," as he says. Although he calls it a little cummie, they don't feel little to me. The waves of orgasm feel big and strong and satisfying and I cannot help but cry out in glorious release. In my current state of denial, just writing about how good it is makes me clench and moisten with need.

He has allowed me to use my fingers and my vibe. Sir finds it particularly amusing when I roll on my tummy on my bed and hump against the vibe, like the wanton slut desperate to get off that I am.

And there's been one other way he's had me come. This one was different and it's only happened once. He's had me come with what he affectionately named "little knobby".

I can't remember how it came up, but at some point

Sir and I became aware that the knob on a desk drawer in my room was at the perfect height for me to press my little pussy against it. Sir wondered if I could get off on it. His wondering and denying me got me to the point where I actually began to look forward to trying, where the little round knob on this drawer began to look good to me. But Sir can be very strict. He forbade me from testing it out, from trying it to see how it would feel. I could only look. And wonder.

Finally he gave me the task. Edge eight times. Then set the timer for two minutes. If I am desperate enough to come on a little knob in two minutes, then I may. If not, I must stop and continue to be denied.

I was so horny I was sure I could come and come easily. The eight edges had me completely wild with lust. I was eager to rub myself to completion. I set the timer. And approached the drawer.

But I quickly realized it wasn't going to be as easy as it looked. The pillow was easy to manipulate and push down on exactly the way I needed to. With this knob, that was not possible. I could only stand and try and thrust against it. There was none of the delicious pressure, none of the control I was used to. I felt my orgasm begin to wane.

I was so desperate, though! I could have cried. I slammed my hands atop the desk, thrust my hips forward and desperately ground myself against that little hard protrusion. God, when I think of how ridiculous I must have looked it is fairly mortifying. Sweating, the tops of my thighs scraping the underside of the drawer, all awkward, knees slightly bent, pelvis gyrating lewdly, moving up and down and forward and back, desperately trying to get the angle and rhythm right to be able to eke out that come. All with the timer ticking!

It goes to show what a horny slut I am that I managed to do it. Even with enough time left to try and hump out some pleasure from the waves of aftershock. I hate to think of the noises I made. It was the bumpiest, gangliest, most desperate, frustrating come I've ever had, only partially satisfying and fully humiliating.

It really fucks with my head that part of me hopes Sir will make me do it again.

MAY 22

I did the cum slut training!

I completed it yesterday. After a long period of denial and then the frustrating little orgasm on the knob, I was felt as desperate and needy as ever. Sir ordered me to hump out 13 orgasms for him, to show what a horny little slut I am. (The way he calls it "humping" makes me so embarrassed … and so wet.) As luck would have it, after a couple of days with lots of privacy to touch and edge myself to complete distraction (seriously, I was like a madwoman, I felt like I would go out of my mind if I wasn't allowed relief), yesterday was a busy day for me with an eight hour shift at work and then lots of errands after. So trying to fit all of my orgasms in, something I didn't even consider while I was denied and completely gagging for a little cummie, ended up being a challenge!

Because of the lack of alone time, at one point I had to cluster four orgasms into a five minute period. When I told Sir this he said he was completely unsurprised at my ability to come over and over. He knows how horny his little pussy is and what it is capable of.

After each I had to say, "Even when I'm a bad little girl, my pleasure is to give Sir pleasure." I admitted to Sir that saying what a bad girl I am during an orgasm makes me come that much harder.

MAY 10

Today at work a kid came in and asked for books on how to draw manga cartoons. I felt this strange little hit of jealousy, like I wished I could go back to that age and start again, knowing that I wanted to draw and not being hindered by ... everything else that happened.

Sir wants to know why I am so reluctant to share my drawings. I think I should explain to him about what happened with HWSN ... with Bill. And Ashley.

Or perhaps it's best to begin with the picture.

Or perhaps this one, which is really the one that started it all.

MAY 11

I had the dream again last night. But this time it was slightly different.

My sleep was disturbed and fitful, plagued with strange images. I was a small girl again, back in Daddy's church. His sermon was fiery and he

loomed larger than life at the front of the church. Delia and I were seated in the front pew as always and our legs dangled high over the floor. So high. I peered over the edge of the pew and it seemed the floor was miles below making me feel dizzy and precarious. Daddy's sermon raged on. As it did, he seemed to grow and I seemed to shrink. His loud voice boomed, "Corinthians 7:34 says 'An unmarried woman or virgin is concerned about the Lord's affairs: Her aim is to be devoted to the Lord in both body and spirit. But a married woman is concerned about the affairs of this world—how she can please her husband.'"

With that he reached a huge, long arm into the front pew where I was sitting. But suddenly I was not sitting there. I was part of the pew. I was a small dark blotch on the backrest of the white pew ... and Daddy was attempting to scrub me out.

MAY 15

What happened with Ashley all started because I took an art course at a local college.

I had talked with Bill about it first. I enjoyed the library and the patrons, I told him, but I wanted something I could feel really passionate about. Though I hadn't really drawn much of anything since I dropped out of my degree, drawing was always the thing I poured my heart into when I was younger. I wanted to get that creative intensity back. Bill told me to go for it.

I met Ashley on the first day. Wise-cracking and charming, so artsy and alternative, I knew immediately I wanted to be friends. Ashley had a brazen level of sexuality that I'd never experienced before. We talked about intimate things and I spilled my guts about my boring and virtually non-existent sex life with Bill. Our conversations blew life into me, shook me up and made me want to step out of the rut I was in. Ashley suggested maybe what Bill and I needed to try was something outside the box, something daring and adventurous to throw a new spark into our sex lives. What could provide that spark? A threesome with Ashley.

I thought about that for weeks. It dominated my thoughts. Three pairs of arms, three pairs of legs, bodies entangled, moving, writhing. It was so forbidden, so wrong but it also seemed wanton and indulgent and so fucking hot. That's when I drew the picture. I didn't even draw it for pleasure. I drew it in order to get it out of my head. The images, the bodies, the pulsing, the heat, they slithered and thrashed and twisted around in my mind and would give me no peace. I drew them to purge them, to purge myself of their all consuming presence.

I drew on autopilot, not even thinking, it just flowed out from the tip of my pencil. When I sat back to really look at it for the first time I was both shocked and amazed by my own daring. The fact that Bill and I were both naked was, for me, risqué enough, since I hadn't drawn another naked body since I'd drawn Bill all those years ago. But the extra set of hands on my body put this work in another category all together.

It was the best thing I'd drawn in years and I wanted Bill to see. I was nervous, unsure of what he would think of the content, worried that he might be angry at what I was imagining. I imagined him laughing derisively at me or being disgusted or worse, just ignoring me. But he did none of those things.

He was intrigued. He wanted to know all about Ashley. So I told him.

To my amazement he seemed excited by the idea of a threesome. My husband, this man who I had never seen show anything but grudging tolerance for anything sexual, was more excited than I'd ever seen him. I started drawing more pictures of the three of us together in all different configurations, bodies intertwined, hands grasping, mouths searching. Bill seemed to love the theme of my new drawings and wanted to see all of them. After we would have sex, talking about Ashley and what the three of us would do to each other. I thought it would be so exciting to have another person's hands on me while I eagerly fucked my husband. And for the first time Bill was engaging with me, looking at me, talking to me, such hot, dirty, filthy words in my ear while we fucked like we had never fucked before.

Oh, I thought it was so hot when Bill suggested he could call Ashley and set up our tryst. I felt so sexy thinking about the experience my husband was going to allow me, anticipating how I would be the centre of attention.

But of course ... the joke was on me. Because when I came home unexpectedly in the middle of that day in December after forgetting my lunch (oh, the cliché of finding the cheating husband at home with his lover in the middle of the day! It makes me want to stab them both with one of those little wooden library pencils for failing to be at least a little original.) I realized that what Bill wanted wasn't a threesome. It was never about the three of us, the way it was for me. What he wanted, what I saw when I walked in, was this:

MAY 26

I have swallowed my pride. I can't take it anymore.

On Skype tonight I begged Sir to come back, even just for a weekend. Or I said I would go there. I didn't know how I'd get the money or the time off of work but I'd swing it somehow. Didn't he want to be together again?

"You know I do, baby girl."

God, what his words do to me! *Baby girl.* The words sunk into my soul, making me bow my head to him, making me still. The endearment made me feel small and owned and loved. I felt like my chest could barely contain my heart inside it. Staring into his eyes I said the thing that has been burning within me, what I felt I couldn't hold back any longer. "I love you, Sir!" I blurted.

His reaction surprised me. He smiled and said, "I love you too, pet," as if he'd known it a long time, known it and accepted it. Accepted it as something to bear.

There was something sad in his eyes.

When I asked him what the matter was, he simply said, "I would love to see you again. Nothing would give me more pleasure. But it's simply not possible. I'm ... needed here." His voice was grim and burdened.

What is keeping him there that he can't leave? A wife? A girlfriend? A child? Why wouldn't he be honest with me when he knows about Nathan?

My sweet Nathan.

Nathan, who is coming home soon.

MAY 29

I feel like I am addicted to play time with Sir. I always come back to it.

Sir asked me to write about when we played on Skype yesterday and, as ever, I'm embarrassed but eager to comply.

After he had put me through the cum slut training, when I felt like my body was drained of all its sexual tension and energy, he got right back to sending me teasing emails. Unbelievably, it caused the sated peace I thought I was enjoying to be unexpectedly short lived. It was as though my body was hard wired to respond to Sir's words. His emails were so 'him' I could practically hear his sexy voice in my head as I read them. In no time at all he had me all ramped up again.

I was really desperate for play time and, as always, for a chance to come for him. So when he said the magic words, "Get your pillow, little girl," I eagerly grabbed it. For something I would have once thought of as horrifyingly shameful, I now jumped gleefully at the chance.

As he edged me I begged him, "please Sir, please. I need to come. Please let me." He kept saying "maybe." To have him say "maybe" is so fucking sexy, it's hard to put into words. I love the power inherent in such an answer. To be held completely at his whim is so intoxicating. To need something so badly and have him airily meet my begging with a simple 'maybe' just makes me burn with desire and lust and the need to be his perfect little girl.

One of his favorite ways to edge me is to make me masturbate while he counts. I have to hold my little cummie for him for a certain length of time that he counts out. Sometimes the counting does me in. I don't know why it's so sexy but it just is and sometimes I have to stop or risk coming without permission.

> *... 8 ... .9 ... hold it for me until 10, little girl*

This time I was able to manage to hold it until 10! And Sir was proud of me. But then he switched to talking to me. Sir knows all of my weaknesses and little buttons to press to challenge me. I had to stop during his talking because, as he said, I "had no control." In fact I had to stop twice because I almost came over the things he said.

> *I have to stop, Sir!*

> *That's my little girl. You know I love to watch you struggle to control yourself for me. Do it just a little bit longer. Come on, show me how you can hold it.*

By this time I was completely desperate. I had edged over and over. I was desperately hoping Sir would let me come. I begged him over and over. He chuckled as he watched me, as he knew from what I'd confessed another time that even the begging makes it hard to control myself, it's so submissive.

Finally he said the words I was so desperate for. He told me I could "come at any time." Which is funny and blush inducing because that sounds as if I might have needed a minute to get there. In fact, no sooner had he said it than I was coming. If Sir is at all in doubt of just how close to the edge I hold myself for him, the fact that I come on command, as soon as he grants permission, should demonstrate it.

Sir likes to chuckle at me because, even though I gave myself lots of little cummies before I met him, he knows none of them are as amazing and powerful and satisfying as the ones where he revs me up to near impossible heights and then releases me. Oh god, to release at Sir's word, to come crashing down after holding back for so long knowing that I do so only for him, is a pleasure that is completely unmatched. The first time I felt it I knew it was the thing I had been waiting for my whole life. I am ever grateful to Sir that he understands me so well and is able to give me exactly what I need.

JUNE 5

I can't believe I'm doing this but I've finally agreed to let Sir submit some of my work to the graphic arts department at the publishing house where he works. He said they are looking for artists and that my work is better than anyone they've got. Of course, he's biased. But I love that he believes in me.

Nathan comes home tomorrow and I don't know what I should tell him. There is still no possibility that I will see Sir, so most of the time I just don't think there is any point in mentioning it. But the fact is, I love Sir. And I love Nathan. I don't know what to do with my feelings for Sir in light of what happens between Nathan and me.

Nathan called me from the airport before his flight today. He wants to come to the cottage as soon as he's home. He said he was a filthy boy and that his mind was filled with nasty thoughts of what he wants to do to my body, what he wants me to do to his. He said he rubbed so many out while he was gone he's actually sore and chafed. He's eager for chastising, for punishment, for humiliation. I marvel at his desire to debase himself before me.

Then I remember what I do with Sir.

Bill is still leaving voicemail messages on my phone. Last night one came in at 3:22 a.m. Curiosity got the better of me and I listened. Bill had obviously been drinking.

Charla -? Char, honey, will you ever take m'callzz? Lissen, I know I lied to you but deep down you had to know. You remember what happen'd when we were kidz, Char. You know what huppend with Dylan. I know you knew. I was always this way. But I juss wan you to know that I never cheated. Not before Ashley. Okay? I wan you know that. You were my bess frien' Char. I luff you. Please talk to me.

I only discovered the message after dinner tonight and when I listened I started shaking all over. I thought I was going to throw up. I lay down for a while ... and fell asleep. Now it's 1:30 a.m.

I wonder if I'll dream of scrubbing church pews tonight, or if it will be the other strange one with Daddy scrubbing.

JUNE 10

If I thought my life was a mess at the beginning of the year I could hardly be prepared for the state it's in now.

Nathan. Oh Nathan. When he came to see me he immediately flung himself at my feet.

"Please Mistress, please." His words came out like a long, low moan. "I've missed you so much. I need your control of me. I need to serve you."

In my head I wasn't where he was, though. I was distracted. I couldn't stop thinking about Sir. When I had told Sir that Nathan was coming home and that maybe I should tell him about us he only laughed. "I don't mind you having playtime with your little toy, pet. I'm not there to physically fulfill your rather significant sexual needs." As he said the word "significant" his eyebrow went up and he looked at me with that knowing and amused stare that always put me in my place. "Just as long as you and I both know to whom your orgasms belong."

"You mean … ?"

"Yes, pet," Sir said. "You may have all the naughty fun you like with your little friend. But you save your baby cummies for me."

The thought of being with Nathan without permission to come simultaneously frustrated and inflamed me.

"I'll enjoy thinking of you engaged in play with that boy and holding your orgasm for me. It will be our fun little secret."

So there was Nathan, prostrated on the floor of the cottage, and for the first time I had no idea what to do with him. He looked up at me with a questioning gaze. "Oh god, I'd forgotten how beautiful you are Mistress." He took my hands, put them on his head and said, "Tell me how I can please you. I'll do anything you desire."

He nuzzled his face into my mound and breathed in deeply. "Fuck," he said, in a tone full of longing. "Your smell. God, how I've missed your smell." He pressed his nose into me harder, his hands on my ass. "Please, please," he murmured into the folds of my skirt. "I need to lick you. I need you on me. I need your taste."

Before I could stop him he had his head under my skirt, his fingers quickly yanking down my panties. He hooked one of my legs over his shoulder and buried his tongue deep inside me. In our time together he'd become much more adept at licking me and as his tongue lapped at my clit and his lips sucked that sensitive nub into his mouth, I felt my legs begin to tremble. I grabbed a hank of his hair in my hand to steady myself on my one leg and prepared to ride my little subbie's face into orgasmic oblivion. Then I caught a glimpse of the ring on my finger.

You save your little cummies for me.

"Oh fuck ... " I called out. Nathan took this as a sign of impending orgasm and started to push his face into me harder. "Oh fuck!! I screamed. "No, Nathan, no," I said, tearing myself away from him.

I stood pushing my skirt back down, my body trembling. My pussy pulsed in aroused frustration. I took a breath and tried to compose myself.

"Mistress, did I do something wrong?" Nathan crawled back towards where I stood.

I managed a weak smile. "No, little boy. That was nice. I just ... didn't want to come just yet."

We continued playing. But I continued to be distracted. Every time I felt that Mistress part of me start to rise up, the part that enjoyed toying with and humiliating and being mean to my little boy, I would think about Sir and feel all that dominance flow away.

I hadn't planned on telling Nathan about Edward. I thought I didn't need to. But when he sat back on my bed, his face contorted with confusion, and said, "Charlotte, what is going on?" I didn't know what else to say.

I have been on that end of a nasty surprise. Granted Nathan and I were not involved in the long term marriage that Bill and I had, but still. I know the hurt of betrayal. Do

I ever. Nathan's reaction, however, astounded me.

He got up from the bed and paced naked around the room, clutching his hair. "So that week before I left, when I hardly heard from you, that was why?"

"Yes," I whispered.

"And you went to see him at his hotel." He stared at me and I couldn't decipher the look in his eyes. "What did you do with him?"

"Nathan … "

"Tell me what you did with him," he said, and his face looked naked with pain. Or so I thought. But soon I realized other emotions were there too.

"We were together," I said tentatively. "We … "

"You fucked," he said. "You fucked him."

And then something in Nathan changed.

He came over to the bed where I was sitting up. He knelt down beside it and looked up at me. "Was he better than me, Mistress?" he asked. His eyes were shiny but when I looked down I was stunned to see that his cock was growing, becoming harder as I watched.

"Nathan." I faltered. "It's not like that."

"Tell me, Mistress," Nathan said grabbing my hand and clasping it between his two. I'd never seen his eyes plead this strongly with me. "Did he satisfy you? He probably could … could … " and he looked down at himself, at his growing erection, and then back up at me with a look so full of shame and lust and humiliation. " … could fuck you a really long time. Not like me."

I saw it then. What Nathan wanted. The depths of his need for complete humiliation. Just how mean he needed me to be to him. I didn't think I could do it. How could I treat him that way?

I saw him read my hesitation. "Did he tell you he's married?" he said.

Sitting here now, alone in the quiet cottage, I am hurt and sad and so confused. And I feel stupid. Of course he's married. Anyone could have picked that up. What else could he have meant by "it's too hard to get away"? Stupid, stupid Charlotte. Blind again.

But in that moment with Nathan, those feelings were in the background. What rose up in me then was Mistress on speed, Mistress times ten, Mistress 2.0.

Anger lit a fire in me. And Nathan got all the meanness that he was so desperate for.

JUNE 20

And still Nathan begs for more. More meanness, more details, more torture. This is an email I sent him.

Aw, you want mean, little boy? Do you? You want to be pushed around and used? You want to be reduced to a little wet mess in the corner with a teeny tiny but very hard cock?

Let's talk about when Edward fucked me then. Because that's what you like, isn't it? The thing that gets you hardest, the thing that makes your cock pulse, the thing that puts that look of pain and lust on your face, is this thought: Another man satisfying me in ways that you can't. I love putting that look on your face, do you know that? I love it when I can see the torment written all over you. It makes me want to push your head down, it makes me want to rise up above you and shove my cunt over your mouth, order you to lick for everything you're worth and make me come in the way that you can with your tongue, even if your pathetic little cock spurts way too fast for me to be able to achieve orgasm.

Edward has a huge cock. Did I tell you that? Yes, little boy, it's huge. Much bigger than yours. Something tells me that you have a twisted little desire to watch just how well he can satisfy me. We could put you in the closet with a gag around your mouth so you don't make any noise and bother me while I'm fucking a real man with a huge cock. I'll leave your hands free so you can stroke your teeny dick while you watch. I know you'll want to do that. But you better fucking hold your cum and not make any fucking mess in there. Because if I come in there and find a mess, oh little boy, you are going to be in so much fucking trouble. There will have to be consequences. First you'll have to come out and show Edward and me how much cum exploded out of your little dick while you were watching him fuck me like you can't because you're a little boy and you just get too excited. Then you'll have to lick your cold jizz off the floor. Make sure the floor is all clean with your tongue while we both watch you on your knees licking.

Eventually he'll have to leave. And I'll tell you to get on the bed. We'll put straps on the bed and I'll tie your hands and legs to it. I'll order you to Be. Fucking. Quiet. You are my fuckstick and I want to fantasize about what just happened with Edward while I use you to masturbate. If your breathing is too loud and interrupts my thoughts I will put my hand over your mouth again. But this time I'll cover your nose as well. You need to shut the fuck up while I'm using you to masturbate because how can I concentrate on my sexy thoughts about a real man like Edward when your breathing is interrupting me?? Aw, you can't breathe? Aw, that's too bad. You should have been quiet like I told you. And don't you even THINK about coming while I am using you, little boy. You are not supposed to be getting any pleasure out of this. You keep your tiny dick hard, don't make any noise and just lie still. That's what you're here for. That's why I keep you around.

Afterward I'll want to relax and read a book. I'll let you go down on me while I read. You can lick me and think about the huge cock that was just stretching me open. You'd like that, wouldn't you, slut?

I think I'll need to smack your cock several times afterward, just to remind you that you are not supposed to be getting so horny from watching some stud fuck me. That's really fucking perverted.

Mistress

JUNE 22

How things change. My solace now is work. Work is where I feel normal. I put on my nice clothes and my nice shoes and my nice smile and I go to work and help people. It makes sense.

Strangely Pig Face is not even annoying me these days. She likes everything in its place. I enjoy putting everything in its place. There is an order in the library and order is good. I used to hate the tedious task of shelving books but these days it's comforting. I find each item's perfect spot. I place it there. I go into a sort of zen-like state.

When the catalog indicates that a book is in and I can't find it, it makes me crazy. It says it's here. Where could it be? Sometimes I'll find books that are missing. I check them back into the catalog and get a lovely sense of satisfaction when the message pops up that a missing item has been found. Ahh. Order. The book is back where it should be.

I shelve things and I try not to think about how much I miss Sir. How much comfort I got from his control of me. How I shared my every thought and fantasy with him and how he strove to make them come true. How he knew exactly the dominance I needed and how he was that for me. How he got me.

It's strange how his very cool, calm, resoluteness that makes me feel safe and secure and submissive to him is the very thing that made me crazy when I confronted him about his wife. He didn't look caught. He didn't look guilty. He didn't break a sweat. He looked very serious, yes, but he was as calm as ever. He said there were some things I didn't understand, that if I took a moment with him, he could explain.

Ah, that old phrase. He could explain? What was he going to explain? That he didn't love her anymore? That they had an 'understanding'? That their marriage was just a sham? I bet that was what Bill said to Ashley. I bet that's exactly what he said. Our marriage was a cover. That I was his 'beard.' All those years I gave to him, all my love, my devotion, the times I desperately wanted him and he was just using me. And now he's tossed me away.

Well, I have about as much time for Edward's bullshit explanations as I have for Bill's. The both of them can go and get fucked.

JUNE 24

To: Charlotte Campbell <ccampbell@pp-lib.com>
From: David Burlow <dburlo@xanderpublishing.com>
Subject: Artwork

Dear Ms. Campbell:

Thank you for submitting your artwork via Mr. Harden for our consideration. We are launching a new line of erotic graphic novels under a separate imprint and we are currently looking for freelance artists. If you would like to be considered we are asking for a one-page treatment in a manga style format with at least seven panels on the page. Explicit content is welcome. Your submission may be in full color or black and white. The deadline for submissions is July 31.

We look forward to hearing from you.

David Burlow
Creative Director

JUNE 25

Another black day. Called in sick to work.
The dream is getting worse.
Can't get out of bed.

JUNE 30

I don't know who I am anymore. When did I become a person who says the horrible things I've said?

At least Delia warned me he was coming. She told me that Bill begged her to let him know where I was staying so she finally relented and told him. She said Ashley left him and that he's been drinking a lot. I guess that accounts for that horrid, drunken voicemail message I got.

Delia said to me, "Charlotte, he probably wants to settle things with you. He said something like that. I mean, you don't want to live in your dad's rundown old cottage forever, do you? If he sells the house and you split the proceeds you could get a nice little townhouse closer to the city, closer to your work. But you have to *talk* to him first. You can't ignore him forever."

I figured that was true.

Once I gave it more thought I decided maybe I was at a place where I could just sort things out with Bill so that we could go our separate ways. We didn't have to talk about the past, I thought. Just deal with the present facts so we could move on. I prepared myself for a straight discussion. Not too friendly but civil enough for us to move to the next step.

When he knocked and I opened the door for him I was shocked when he grabbed me and hugged me.

"Charlotte! Oh honey, I didn't think you'd let me in. Thank god. It feels so good to hold you again." I wriggled away from him and stepped back, frowning. "Okay, I get it," Bill said. "I get that it's going to take time. I'm just so happy to see you."

I looked around, feeling very awkward. "Uh, do you want a drink?" I asked, heading for the kettle in the kitchen.

"Yes! A nice glass of cab sav would be perfect."

He was sitting on the couch staring at me. Suddenly I felt like I didn't know what to do with myself. My arms seemed to hang in a strangely awkward way beside my body. I stood in the little cottage kitchen waiting for the kettle to boil.

I put his wine down at the small wooden kitchen table and sat down with my tea. After a moment he stood up from the couch and came over.

"I guess now I should say what I came to say," Bill said, sitting. I furrowed my brow. It was six months since I'd seen this man who, before that horrific moment when I found him with Ashley, I used to see everyday of my life. It was so strange to be in a room with him again. He looked different. I didn't recognize the shirt he was wearing. His face looked gray and gaunt. He seemed jumpy and unsettled. I thought, is telling me he wants to sell the house this difficult?

"I assume Delia told you that Ashley's gone," he said. I winced inwardly hearing Bill say Ashley's name but nodded. Bill gulped down half the glass of red in one swig then blurted out the last thing I ever thought I'd hear him say. "Charlotte, I want you to come back home."

At first I was just confused. I thought he was suggesting that the two of us live our separate lives under one roof. So I just laughed and told him not to be silly, that surely we'd get enough from the sale of our house to be able to manage our own separate accommodations. Maybe not as large but what did it matter?

But then he started to talk about how it was all a big mistake. That Ashley was a mistake. After Ashley had left he was so lonely, he'd gone to see his family. They helped him. They made him see. He was just confused. He was confused *then*. But he said he knew what he wanted now. It was me. He'd been a fool, an idiot, a blind imbecile. He missed me so much. Wouldn't I come home where I belonged, with him, as his wife.

I sat stunned for a few moments. Then slowly I stood. My body was vibrating with rage. I could feel the bile bubbling inside of me. I wanted to smack him, smack that stupid fake forlorn look off his face. Instead I grabbed what was left of the wine and hurled it at him.

And then I let go of a torrent of hate.

"How dare you," I said. "How fucking dare you!"

"Charlotte ... " he began.

"No! You listen now, Bill," I said, glaring at him.

"Now it's YOUR turn to listen.

"You lie to me for our entire marriage, you reject me over and over until I have no self esteem left, you cheat on me with my friend, you force me to go and live like some pauper in this run down shack while you stay in our home with Ashley, butt fucking each other's brains out ... "

Charlotte? a voice inside me asked.

" ... and now you want me to come *back*?? What, so you can do it all again? Once wasn't good enough? All those years of ignoring me, of *tolerating* me, that shit wasn't cruel enough for you? You need to fuck with me some more?" I stood staring at him and panting. "How much of an *idiot* do you take me for?"

I gasped for breath and stomped around the cottage. I couldn't stand still. I had to move, there was so much rage and indignation inside me I felt like flailing my limbs about to try and dispel it.

"And then you have the nerve to call me and tell me that 'deep down I knew.' Because of what happened when we were kids? I assume you're talking about when you literally got caught with your pants down with Dylan Fergus. What about all the times you told me that I was really the one, that what happened with Dylan was just a silly case of boys will be boys, that you really wanted me. Do you remember that Bill? You said those things to me over and over. Until we were married, that is," I said, sneering and sweating.

I needed it out, all the hurt and anger were too much

for me to bear. And in that moment, I realized all that I had were words, all that could help purge the horrible swirl of negativity inside me were words. So I reached for the most cutting ones I could find.

"Tell me, what happened when you went back home to your family this time? You know, I can almost forgive you for succumbing to your father's tyranny then. We were young after all. But now? What could he have said to you now? What could he have said to make you come back here and try to convince me to embark on another journey of hurt, of lies, of rejection? What did he do? Did he shame you? Did he call you names? How's this for a name: LYING FUCKING FAGGOT!"

Charlotte?

I didn't care. I screamed it at him, screamed as loud as I could, and then ordered him out of the house.

Charlotte? the voice is asking me still, as I sit here now. Who is the person who would scream such hateful things at someone who is so obviously confused and in pain?

I didn't know. I was lost. And all I could think of was how I wanted Sir.

July 1

Dear Sir,

I need you so badly. I miss you so much.

You may think it's rash that I blocked your email address at work, or that I closed the email account I was using exclusively to communicate with you. I couldn't bear to keep lines of communication open. I wouldn't have been able to stop myself from reading any message you might send.

Deleting the account caused me actual physical pain. I felt it in my gut. I sobbed, wrenching wails like I've never cried before, not when my marriage was over, not when my father died, not ever. It scared me. All of our beautiful words to each other ... gone. I guess it is the digital world version of burning all your letters and it hurt me, Sir. It hurt me so much. But I had to.

You're married.

I just can't continue this with you.

I torture myself with opening Skype to see if your little green check mark is lit up. If it is though, after a fleeting feeling of happiness knowing you're there, I quickly go offline.

But you're inside me. You're with me in my heart constantly. I can cut off our actual communication Sir, but what if I can't stop talking to you in my head? I don't know what to do with myself. I feel out of my mind with wanting you, wanting your words, wanting to tell you things. So I'm writing to you here because I just don't know what else to do.

We were only together that once. But god, how the memory of your touch fuels me. I remember the very first moment our bodies made contact, did you know that? You put your hand on mine when we were downstairs at your hotel. Just that one small touch but I felt it through my whole body, through my whole being.

There was a moment, Sir, when I took off every bit of clothing for you and you saw my body for the first time. I saw your Dom defenses go down. Maybe you didn't know, but I saw. You caressed me and knelt before me and held me. I could see afterward that you corrected yourself for momentarily losing your cool. But Sir, that was the moment I fell in love with you. I love when you control me, I love when you instruct me, I love when the raise of your eyebrow makes me wet. But that brief moment of weakness felt like a kind of submission to me and it was when my heart first opened up to you.

I looked at my ring just now and I realized something. Yin and Yang are very much complimentary forces. They don't work against each other but in harmony to create a result. There is a bit of each that resides in the other. That is why they fit so well together. They actually have a part of the other within them. When you saw me naked for the first time I saw the white dot of my yang swimming in your black yin. And I fell in love.

I love all of you, Edward. And you're not mine to love.

I wonder things. Sometimes I think I'll go mad with wondering.

I wonder how you could do it. How could you lie to her? To me? I feel so stupid. I thought you were the kind of man to make promises and keep them. I felt that from you. I guess I was wrong.

I wonder if you hold her at night and think of me.

I wonder if you make love to her and think of that night in your hotel when you made me yours. I wonder, when you feel her pulse around you as she orgasms, if you remember how I held mine for you, only letting it go when you said.

Or maybe she is your submissive too. That's who you were talking about when you mentioned your "RL play." Maybe she obeys you. Maybe you were dominating her too the whole time, just tossing out orders to this one and that one. Maybe you call her pet also, that just made it easier to dish out commands. God, the thought of someone else being your pet is a pain that's almost too much to bear.

I wonder what she looks like. I wonder what she calls you. I wonder what made you go outside of your marriage to find me. I wonder if you even care now that I'm gone.

Perhaps I was just a passing diversion for you. Perhaps you do this all the time, find horny little subs to have a fun little fling with and then move on. Perhaps.

But I just want to write down here that it wasn't that for me, Sir. For me it was something special, something I'd never experienced, something beautiful. And even though it kills me sometimes, I still wear the ring you gave me that symbolizes my submission to you.

Because, even though you are not mine, in my heart I know I

will always be yours.

　　With undying love,

　　pet

July 4

　　LEVITT, HENRY *Contemplating Divorce: Should You Stay?*
Ha. Knew it.

　　I want to write a little note on LEVITT, HENRY's hold
slip. *Of course you shouldn't stay. She's probably fucking somebody
else anyway.* Everybody cheats.

　　Including me.

　　Today I'm scheduled to do
a shift back here with Fritz. I tossed
him a glance as I walked into the
Dungeon and he blinked his light at
me as if to say, "You again, huh?"

　　With our reacquaintance out of the way, we
got on with our business, him gulping down books and
farting them out into bins and me yanking them out again.
Hey, that's what it's like! They're like book farts.

　　　　　　　　　　　　I'm the person who
　　　　　　　　　　　　collects book farts.

Charlotte Campbell
Book Fart Collector

It is very quiet in the library today. Fritz's bins are all emptied out and we are both just sitting here, eying each other suspiciously. Pig Face is away today, thank god for small mercies, so this is a perfect opportunity for me to work on my submission to Xander Publishing. I told Delia about it at dinner last night.

"Char, that's amazing!" she said.

"Yep," I said, circling the top of my wine glass with my finger.

"Why haven't you told me sooner? Aren't you excited? People submit and submit and wait ages for anyone to notice their work. You have an in!"

"I know, Dee. I am excited. It's just, I'm having some trouble … producing."

"What are you talking about? What about all the sketches in your diary? Just use those," Dee said, staring intently across at me.

I let out a big sigh.

"Wha-aat?" Dee said. She looked like she was ready to reach across and shake me.

"No, I know. It's fine. I'm just frustrated." She kept staring at me expectantly. "I can't use those sketches, Dee!"

"Why not? The one you showed me was excellent. I told you, your best work."

"No, it's not the work. I feel good about the quality of that drawing … ." I took a french fry and started breaking it into pieces.

"Then what the hell is the problem?" Dee said.

I sat back in my chair and lifted my eyes to the ceiling, rubbing the side of my face. "Because *I'm* in them!"

Dee scoffed. "Charlotte, come on. Nobody will know it's you," she said.

"They might! What if they decide to publish those ones and work sees them? What if my *mother* does? Oh fuck." I took a gulp of wine and used both hands to rub at my face. "It's just not an option. I have to do something new."

So here I am. The beginning of a very quiet shift that has six hours left in it. No Pig Face. Lots of time to draw.

Here I go.

Don't try and stop me.

JULY 10

I have the day off.

I've turned off my phone and stuck it in a drawer. I hid my laptop under my bed. I unplugged the wireless router and stuck it in the closet for good measure.

I'm going to sketch. I'm going to! That's all there is to it.

I'll just switch the television on. It's good to have something on in the background. The silence is what's killing me.

Fuck.

JULY 15

I'm in Daddy's church. But I'm not as young this time. I'm older.

Bill is there.

Bill's in church and he's naked! *Bill, put some clothes on!* I try and scream but nothing comes out. He just smiles at me.

You're my best friend, Char. Let's try it.

Bill, Daddy's coming.

Then I'm scrubbing again. Scrubbing the pew, scrubbing, scrubbing. I have to make it clean. It won't come out. It won't come out. It's tarnished forever. Tarnished.

JULY 22

Right, let's stop messing around now. I've had my breakfast, my coffee. I went out for a nice, brisk walk to clear my head. I have three hours before I have to leave for work. Plenty of time to get some good quality drawing time in.

Here we go.

Keeping the TV off this time! That was a mistake.
Okay.

Maybe I'll put my iTunes on random. Some music
would be nice.

JULY 25

Nathan showed up on my doorstep tonight.

I admit, I wanted to be gutless and not let him in, pretend I wasn't here, not face what I've done to him. It's terrible the way I've treated him. I know it is. But I couldn't hide from him anymore.

I opened the door. I couldn't believe what I saw.

Nathan!

It's only been about six weeks since I've seen him but I wouldn't have recognized the person that stood in front of me then if he'd passed me on the street.

His glasses were gone. His eyes looked vibrant, a piercing blue, and his gaze looked intent and fiery.

He'd cropped his hair. All that floppy, disheveled hair that made him look so young was now cut short and stood up in spikes that poked this way and that.

He hadn't shaved. Scruffy, tawny, stubble now surrounded those beautiful red lips, taking away that slightly feminine look.

But most strikingly he'd bulked up. He had already started to, after his months lifting and planting trees in the wilderness but nothing like he was now. I didn't know what power drinks he'd been drinking or how many hours he had spent at the gym since I last saw him but the result was astounding. He was wearing low-slung denim shorts and a thin olive green t-shirt and his chest and arms bulged out, the fabric of his tee stretching around his biceps, his calves looking muscled and sinewy.

He stood in the doorway with none of his usual pleading looks. He appeared almost defiant. For a moment I was slightly scared.

"Charlotte," he said, and even his voice sounded deeper. "I need to talk to you. Can I come in?"

I let him in. He paced around a moment while I sat on the couch and stared up at him. I couldn't think what to say. The difference in his appearance was so remarkable. He looked like he'd grown about an inch. Suddenly the adolescent was gone and in his place was this body that was all muscle and testosterone and ... man. He looked like he could have stepped out of the pages of GQ. I was spellbound. But a part of me couldn't help feeling a little twinge of longing for the sweet boy who's eyes filled with tears the first time he was inside me.

"You look really ... different," I said. "Good! I mean, you look great, Nathan."

He smiled, a little shyly, and for a moment my sweet boy was there again.

I took a breath. "Listen, Nathan, I'm really sorry—" I started.

"No, you don't need to apologize," he said. "I was all fucked up there for a while. I ... went somewhere dark. And took you with me. I'm the one who's sorry."

"God, you can't be here apologizing to me after the way I treated you," I said.

He stopped pacing and came and sat down next to me. "Charlotte, school is starting again for me in less than a month. I just want to know before I start back … if you'll be with me again. No, listen, before you say anything, I mean really be with me, like a regular couple. No more Mistress, no more humiliation. I don't need that stuff, Charlotte. I just need you."

He leaned towards me and kissed me then. His stubble prickled into my face and it didn't feel like I was kissing Nathan, not my Nathan. I reached up to grab his hair and felt nothing before I remembered that it was short now. I touched my hand to the top of his head and felt the spikes, all stiff with product. He put his hand on my knee and I jumped. His sweet timidity was all gone and it startled me. I broke the kiss.

He smiled at me but then frowned. "What is it?" he said. "Is it … Edward?"

I looked into my lap. "I haven't seen Edward at all. I mean, we haven't talked or communicated."

"Charlotte, I'm sorry I mentioned his wife when I did."

"What?" I said, looking at him. "No Nathan, I'm glad you did. I had to know."

He got up and started his pacing again. "Well then you should also know that he's never going to leave her, if that's what you're thinking. When he was at my house that night for dinner, he'd had a couple of drinks and my dad asked about her. He said something like, "What kind of a man would I be, to leave my wife after what she's been through." So you see? He's not here, Charlotte, and he never will be. But I am."

We ended up in bed. It was warm and tender, sweet kisses and slow caresses. He moved on top of me and the bulk of him, the physicality was a bit overwhelming. I looked up at him and gasped at the sight of his broad chest flexing above me. I grasped onto his straining biceps and almost swooned. When he pressed himself into my wet folds I braced myself for his usual moan and shudder … but it didn't come. Instead he moved inside me, holding me, kissing me, working me with his body until I cried out and clung to him, pushing my body up to meet his, hungrily seeking out every last spasm.

"I love you, Charlotte," Nathan whispered. I felt his cock pulse, he thrust into me hard, and he came.

"I love you too, sweet boy," I whispered back, kissing his cheek and caressing the short bristles of hair that were now at the back of his head, as his body became still on top of me.

He's gone now. It was a wonderful night. And yet as I sit here writing, I can't help but wonder.

What happened to Edward's wife?

July 27

I'm aware that what happened last night with Nathan would probably not be a big deal to most people. But for me it was something. Something I'd never experienced before.

We were in bed together, just kind of rolling around, touching, talking. He was telling me about where he had been tree planting.

"Hey, I know that area. I used to spend summers up around there as a kid, with my parents," I said. "We would rent the same place every year. It was small but cosy. It had a dock and we would go out on a boat and fish." We were lying facing each other and I was idly stroking his leg.

"It's far, don't you think?" he asked, smiling at me and caressing my arm, running a finger down one side of my breast. "I mean, I thought it was a long trip to get up there." He stuck a leg out and slipped it between my two.

"Mm-mm," I replied, shrugging, thinking about tall pines whipping by the half opened window of the car as I sat in the backseat, the wind making my hair fly in all directions.

"Doesn't it feel long to you?" he asked.

I thought about those trips, Daddy and mama in the front, and how sometimes we'd listen to the country radio stations mama liked, sing along to all the songs, and the trip would just fly by. But sometimes Daddy made us listen to stations like the Fellowship for Christ that didn't even play faith based songs, just shouted fire and brimstone all day, and then the trip seemed to take forever.

"Sometimes yes, sometimes no," I said.

He grinned at me. "I wasn't talking about the drive." He pulled me to him and I felt his hardness in my belly.

"Oh!" I said, giggling. "Oh, well in that case … " I paused, thinking. "Same answer!"

He laughed out loud and rolled on top of me. "And

what about now?" he said, pushing inside me.

I groaned as he slid into me, filling me up. But then I thought about his question and couldn't help but giggle again. "Yeah, I guess it's okay now," I said and burst into laughter.

Then we were rolling around, groaning, laughing, pushing, holding. When it was all done and we were lying in a mess of twisted sheets, sweating and smiling, I looked at him. "That was amazing," I whispered.

His boyish face was all cute, bashful charm and I adored him for it, even if I could tell he didn't really understand quite what I meant, just how amazing it was for me. How could he? These experiences with me were his first. Whereas my sexual history had more ... hard miles on it.

That was the thing. They were hard. And not in the good way. Arduous. Daunting. Disheartening.

One thing it never, ever was, was light hearted. There was certainly never any laughing. Not even close.

So this time with Nathan, to be rolling around together, to actually have him inside me and at the same time be smiling and laughing and happy ... it was like being set free.

July 30

Nothing like leaving things down to the wire. I've gotta draw something today. Something good. Something really hot. The hotness used to just pour out of me. It came right out of the tip of my pencil, like, like ... like cum!

I can do it. I just have to think sexy thoughts.

I'll think about Nathan. Nathan and his new sexy body.

Damn it! I can't do it!

I'm shit. I can't draw for shit. The other times were just a fluke. I can't do this.

If I can't come up with anything then … . No, I can't use my other drawings. I just can't.

AUGUST 5

HAPPY BIRTHDAY TO ME!

It's been a rough year but I think things are on the way up. I'm out of the Dungeon. I like my job again. I have a totally sexy boyfriend who is thankfully interested in having sex with women, particularly me. And I'm sure any time now I'm going to be able to start drawing properly again. I think that deadline really messed with my head and put me in a bit of a rut. But I'll have it behind me soon, I know it.

And guess what? To celebrate, tonight I'm going on a double date!

Delia and Sebastian got a sitter and Nathan and I

are meeting them at Gino's. Yes! It's going to be fun. And not awkward at all. Dee promised me. She said she's over the age thing.

Speaking of age, I'm not going to say a damn thing about how I'm inching closer and closer to forty. Thirty-eight means I'm still in my thirties. I'm going out tonight with my hot, young boyfriend and my dear friends. We're going to have drinks! Oh yes, I'm definitely in the mood for a nice glass of wine tonight. Maybe some bubbly. Woohoo! Nathan's on his way here to pick me up. There he is at the door now!

AUGUST 6

The room … spinning. My head. Oh god, my head.

Good god, help me. I'm never drinking again.

Ever!!

AUGUST 10

When there is a hold for my boyfriend on the hold shelf, how can I resist checking? Who could blame me?

Usually it's just a little passing amusement, a bit of nostalgia from when he put that masturbation book on hold. Last week he ordered season one of *Game of Thrones.*

"Seriously? Season one?" Mel said. "Where the hell has he been?" We had a chuckle.

One time it was *Older Women, Younger Men: How to Get and Keep a Cougar.* Mel and I had a real laugh about that. "Is he trying to get another one?" Mel teased. "Or is he just figuring out how he can keep you around?"

But today. Today it was this:

CURTIS, NATHAN P. *Understanding the Cuckold Mind*

I flicked through a few of the pages.

In the 21st century, cuckoldry is a fetish in which a man eroticizes sexual infidelity …

… a variant of masochism, the cuckold derives pleasure from being sexually humiliated …

… any feeling can become sexualized if it is somehow favorably associated with sex …

Is Nathan still thinking about what happened between Edward and me?

Why?

Does this mean he's not happy with our sex life? I thought our sex life was really good! Okay, maybe it's not as hot as when we first got together. No relationship can stay super hot forever, right? It's just natural for things to sort of

… even out a bit. That's all. But it's still good. I mean, it's nice. It's … cuddly. Comfortable. Normal. Normal is good. Normal is what I want. It's better than it was before, really.

Here's an example of how things are better now. That little problem Nathan used to have, you know, lasting? No longer an issue! It's all smooth sailing. It's great to be able to have an orgasm with him inside me. That never would have happened before because he always got too excited. Now, he's … you know … less excited.

Hmm.

Anyway, it's not like I miss that part of our relationship. The teasing, the humiliation, the meanness … . What normal person would miss inflicting that? That would just be … weird. To miss a thing like that.

August 22

Oh fuck. FUCK!

I … I can't even write. I have to call Delia! Okay, I'm going to call Delia first.

I talked to Delia but it didn't help. I'm still fucking freaking OUT!

Xander Publishing wants to use my work in their graphic novel. Not just any graphic novel, their lead novel to introduce the imprint, which they are calling *Red Ink*. They want to set me up with their writer so we can start brainstorming the rest of the book but they specifically said they want to see it stem from the one page treatment I submitted.

This cannot be happening!!

When I told Delia she thought I was overreacting.

"Charlotte, calm down," she said. "It's going to be fine. Better than fine. This is wonderful news. Your work is being published in a book! This is what you've always dreamed of. You'll be making money from your artwork."

"But Dee, you don't understand! I used MY drawings. I mean, of course I used my drawings. But I used the ones from my diary!"

"I thought you said you weren't going to use those … ." Dee said, frowning.

"I wasn't!" I'm exasperated. I know it's not Dee's fault but I want to shake her. "I wasn't going to. But I had to. I couldn't draw anything else. Everything else I tried to do was shit."

Dee sighed. "Okay. Well, there you go. You've done it now." She shrugged. "The point is they liked it. They liked your work. This is a good thing! You're on your way."

"No, not like this, Dee. Not this work. God, why couldn't I draw endangered animals, like you do?"

"Artists draw what moves them. What they feel passionate about. This is it for you." She grabbed my hand. "You need to stop fighting this. Embrace it, Char. Be proud." She patted my hand. "It's really good work."

She doesn't understand.

No one understands.

AUGUST 30

The dream. The dream again.

I have to get the spot out. It's the whole church. The

whole church is tarnished. Daddy is going to see. I have to get it out.

I scrub and scrub. I get smaller and smaller. Daddy is coming.

What is this spot? What's on here? It's a drawing of a man. A naked man.

Oh, that's naughty!

I am so small. Daddy is big.

You will tarnish the image of the church!

I reach to start scrubbing again but I can't. I am on the pew. I am the spot. Daddy's big hand reaches out ... .

And then I woke up, gasping and shaking.

SEPTEMBER 1

At Gino's tonight I spoke to Dee about the dreams.

"They are really more like nightmares," I told her. "I wake up with my heart pounding. I'm all sweaty, my mouth is dry."

"What about when we used to scrub the church pews is scary?"

"I know, it's dumb."

"No, Char. I don't mean it like that. I mean, what's scary in the dream."

I thought about it a while. "I have this feeling like, I won't get them clean. There is this enormous pressure. I must get them clean and I'm afraid that I won't." Even describing it to Dee, fully awake, there at Gino's, my forehead was clammy.

"What are you afraid will happen if you don't?" Dee asked.

I blotted my napkin on my forehead and took a sip of wine. "I don't know, exactly." I chewed half heartedly on a cold bit of panzerotti. After a moment I remembered something. "I think I've figured out that I seem to have that dream whenever I am worried about showing my sketches to someone new," I said.

"Well, let's talk about that," Dee said. "When was the first time you showed someone a sketch?" she asked. She was picking through what was left of the fries. I felt distracted by my uncomfortably full tummy.

"I don't know, exactly. It was probably Mum, you know, some picture I did at school and brought home to her or something." Even though I was full I couldn't help but pick at the fries too.

"That doesn't sound too traumatic. Ah, but you are all freaky about the content of this current work. So maybe it's a symbolic thing. Maybe the church symbolizes authoritarian morality and you feel guilty about the nature of the content of your work."

"Maybe," I said. I wasn't sure I wanted to talk about it anymore.

"So when was the first time you ever showed someone a drawing that was more ... explicit?"

Suddenly I could feel the panzerotti that I had

wolfed down churn in my stomach.

"Char, are you okay? You look pale. Here, have some water."

I took a sip and my phone buzzed. "Fuck, it's Bill." I put my head down on the table.

"Charlotte," Delia said. She got up from her side of the booth and moved across to sit next to me. She took one of the cloth napkins, dunked it in the water glass and gently lifted my head, smoothed my hair back and wiped the cool cloth across my clammy forehead. I felt my throat constrict and she put her arms around me.

Delia is the kind of friend who I can sit in a restaurant with and cry. Driving home through the darkened streets I thought more about what Dee asked me. About the first time someone saw an explicit drawing of mine. As I sit here in Daddy's cottage the meaning of the dream is becoming clearer. I need to talk to someone about it. Someone who understands me. Who gets me.

I need Sir.

September 5

I had to come to the staff room and take a moment. I'm shaking.

I noticed this hold on the hold shelf:

HARDEN, EDWARD *Coping with Stroke: A Spouse's Guide*

At first all I saw was his name and I started looking all around, as though he might be standing right behind me like the first time. But of course, he wasn't.

Then I saw "stroke" and I immediately thought

he'd had a stroke. But that didn't make any sense.

Obviously this is what he meant when he talked with Nathan's dad about what his wife had been through. She's had a stroke.

Okay.

But why is this book here? Does this mean he's in town? He must be, or he would have just ordered this book at home.

From the back cover:

Stroke can happen at any age. Research shows that many survivors are relatively young as are their spouses. Strokes have a profound effect on relationships, especially that of the spouse turned caregiver. If you are the spouse of a stroke survivor, this guide helps to address many of the physical, psychological, social, emotional and sexual issues a stroke can raise.

Edward, what have *you* been through?

SEPTEMBER 6

Dinners with Dee used to be fun and light-hearted affairs. They really were. You'd never know it from how this year has gone though. Tonight was just another example.

"I don't know what I'm supposed to think," I said. My bowl of udon sat in front of me largely untouched. After I almost tossed up my panzerotti at Gino's the last time, we decided to go for Japanese. "His wife is sick so that means it's okay that he cheated? Isn't that worse? If he's so unhappy why doesn't he leave her?"

"I don't know, Char," Dee said, chasing around a block of tofu with her chopsticks. "These things are complicated."

"He's young to be dealing with this," I said. "I guess he married someone quite a bit older than he is."

"Maybe but not necessarily," Dee said. "We have a guy at Shady Oaks, Eddie. He's 36."

"Really?" I said. "You never told me that."

"Yeah, it's really sad. Perfectly healthy guy. Married, a kid. One day he just had a stroke."

"Oh my god, that's awful," I said. "And he's in a nursing home at 36? What happened to his wife?"

"Nothing. Janet's lovely. She brings their son Ethan to visit him every week."

"Wow," I said. I sat for a moment, taking that in. "Does Eddie have physical disabilities from the stroke?"

"Some," Dee said. "Reduced mobility in one leg. A little bit of paralysis on one side of his face. But you probably wouldn't notice it at first." She grinned and shoved a cucumber roll in her mouth. "Eddie can be a charmer," she mumbled from behind a hand.

"Surely his wife could manage him at home then," I said. "How could she just dump the father of her child in a nursing home at 36? That's terrible."

Delia stared at me. "Listen to what you're saying, Char. A moment ago you asked if Edward was so unhappy why doesn't he just leave. Stroke survivors need care, sometimes a lot. Leaving means you have to arrange that. And some people do, like Eddie's wife. But some people can't manage the guilt. Especially when they come up against attitudes like what you just expressed." I shifted in my seat and looked around. We were both silent a moment. Dee picked up a slice of pickled ginger, looked at it and put it back down. "Stroke changes people," she said. "Sometimes significantly. Usually significantly." She picked up her wine glass and swirled it around, staring at the liquid. "They're angry. They're irritable. And a lot of the time they are completely focused on themselves. The world revolves around them and what their needs are. It is really hard on the spouse."

I knew the thing I wanted to ask her. I felt stupid and petty and selfish for asking but I couldn't help but think about it. "Can they still, you know, have sex?"

"Can they?" Dee said. "I think often they probably physically can. But do they? That's another question."

"What do you mean?" I said.

"Well, take Eddie, for example. He's a pretty attractive guy. He's about my age. I told you he's a charmer. But would I want to have sex with him? I bring him his meals. I give him his meds. I make sure he does his physio. I deal with him when he doesn't want to go to speech therapy. Last week he called me a "fucking cunt" because I told him he had to turn the tv volume down."

"What?" I was horrified. "I thought you said he was a charmer?" I said.

"He is," Dee said, apparently changing her mind about the ginger and popping it in her mouth. "But he has mood swings. He can turn on a dime." She munched thoughtfully. "So would I want to have sex with him? No. And especially not if I were caring for him 24/7, and not as my job but as his wife. Lots of people in that situation don't feel like a spouse anymore. It changes the relationship dynamic.

"They are no longer like husband and wife. They are like patient and carer."

Then I remember Edward's words. *It's simply not possible. I'm … needed here.*

SEPTEMBER 8

I had my first meeting with Xander's writer, Stefan, this morning.

I was all nervous about being identified as the person depicted in my work so I wore baggy clothes, threw my hair in a messy ponytail and wore my glasses instead of putting my contact lenses in. I think I just ended up looking like a grubby, unemployed, starving artist.

But either it worked or it didn't matter because Stefan didn't bring it up. I guess, how could he? It would be hard to stop in the middle of a creative meeting and say hey, by the way, is that you jerking off a guy in the alleyway?

Anyway, I think it went well. We set September 25 for our next meeting and I have a bunch of sketches to do in the meantime around the idea of "a man comes home from work." Lots of leeway there! The only problem is … I haven't sketched anything significant in months. Like Austin Powers, I feel like someone's stolen my mojo.

Well, I don't see how that's going to help me with Stefan.

In any case, that gives me just under three weeks to come up with something. If I'm going to do this I've got to get used to working with deadlines. I'll just have to. I must force myself to draw.

Oh well, right now it's time for work. Then a quiet night in with Nathan tonight. Maybe we'll watch a DVD. Oh, I know! The latest season of *Downton Abbey* came in at work for me yesterday. Since I don't have a PVR at the cottage I haven't seen an episode of *Downton Abbey* in ages. Woohoo! Love Downton.

SEPTEMBER **20**

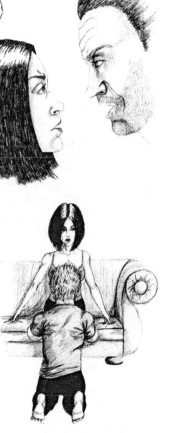

I'm looking for my hold.
The last name is Harden

I didn't know how else to
communicate with you. I ordered that
book as a way of trying to explain
my situation. But then, when I got
the notification that it came in, I had
to come. I know it's not fair of me
to be here. I only have two days. I'll
leave if you want me to but I just
had to see you again.

Please let me watch you, Mistress.
It's true what you said in that email.
I want to watch. You know I do. I
thought it was bad for me to want this
but I've read about it. Lots of other
men are like I am. I want to watch
you have sex with him.

Wow. I think this last one is … good. I think it's really good. I'm back. I got my mojo back!

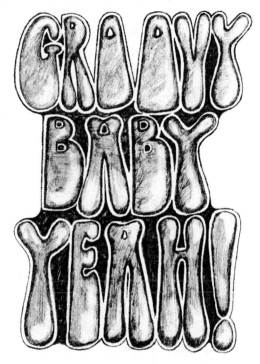

I could even send this to Xander.

SEPTEMBER 22

When I didn't show up for work it was Bill who came to the cottage. I guess I still have him as my contact person at work.

He said he knocked and knocked and when he got no answer, he remembered the key that we always kept underneath the gnome in the front garden. He let himself in.

He found me in the bedroom in the dark, curtains pulled, covers over me. When I saw his face I hugged him and cried.

I started ranting, my words spilling out between sobs. "The dream. The dream came back. Oh god, I sent that drawing of Sir and Nathan and me in to Xander. Why? Why did I do that? I'm so ashamed. The shame is eating at me!" I pulled at my hair and Bill grabbed at my hands. "That night I had the dream again. It was worse than ever." I clutched at the covers and curled myself into a ball, moaning. "He's trying to scrub me out, Bill. I'm the spot. I'm tarnishing his reputation with the church."

"Charlotte honey, what are you talking about?"

I sat up. My head felt thick and hot. "I remember now. When we were kids. Remember our deal? You were trying to get me to sleep with you."

He gave his head a little shake, like he was trying to clear up all the thoughts I was throwing at him. "When we were kids? Why are you—"

"Just … just go with me a minute," I said. "Remember, it was summer. You'd just turned 19 and I was still 18. You said to me, Char, we are both virgins and we both want to know what it's like. Remember? You said it would be okay since we loved each other. So why not try it together."

He bowed his head. "Of course I remember." He sighed. "It was right after the incident with Dylan, after my dad, well, you know how he reacted, you said it before.

But Charlotte, it wasn't a total lie. I meant it when I said I loved you. I still do. We were best friends, inseparable. Look, it's good I'm here now. I've been wanting to talk to you anyway. I'm so sorry—"

"No, it's okay. It's not about that." I put my hand on his arm. "Do you remember what you promised me if I agreed to us having sex?"

He thought for a moment. "You wanted to sketch me, right?"

"Naked," I said.

He smiled. "Naked." He looked pensive. "Naked, 18 year old me, huh? I wouldn't mind seeing that again. Do you still have it somewhere?"

"No," I said quietly. I started to cry again.

"Hey, hey. What's this? Charlotte, what is going on? What's the matter with you?"

And then it all came gushing out.

"Daddy found that picture I drew. I hid it but he went through my things, he used to do that, and he found it. He said it was filth. He said he knew what I'd done with you. I'd fornicated out of wedlock and I was disgusting." I let out a sob, remembering how it felt to have my father fling that word at me. But then I pushed on. "He tore the picture up in front of me and then he slapped me. Hard. Across my face." I put my hand on my cheek. "He said I better make this right or having a slut for a daughter would tarnish his reputation with the church. He told me I had to marry you."

Bill sat looking stunned. "So we both got married to please our fathers." We stared at each other.

We sat together for a long time after that. Bill made us cups of tea and he called work for me and said I'd gotten the flu and couldn't get out of bed. He brushed my hair and blotted at my weepy red eyes with tissues and we talked for hours. It was like when we were kids. We were inseparable then, like he said. We would stay up all night on the phone. Even when we first were married we could talk for ages, before the resentment towards each other built up. We were best friends. I did love Bill. And he loved me. We were just never meant to be lovers.

"I'm so sorry for screaming at you when you were here before," I said. "What I called you, I don't even know where that came from. I don't use language like that. It was inexcusable."

His eyes were soft and warm. "Apology accepted. And the yelling was necessary. I can't believe I almost let my dad do that to me again. That I considered doing that to you again. You had every right to be furious. And you were right. I was afraid. Even with Ashley I was afraid, pretending to be bi, pretending that all I wanted was a little spice in our marriage when deep down I knew I was lying to you."

"You were lying to yourself, Bill."

"I was," he said. "But not anymore." A huge grin lit up his face.

"My goodness! Bill Campbell, what is that smile

for?" I said.

For a moment his smile faded. "Uh, I don't know if this is weird for me to be telling you this but ... I met someone."

I thought about it. *My husband has just told me he's met someone.* "You know what?" I said finally. "Weirdly," I paused, realizing it as I was saying it. "Weirdly, it doesn't feel weird at all." We hugged again. "Tell me all about him."

SEPTEMBER 23

My dearest Sir,

How I miss you. I think about you constantly. When you managed to visit here two weeks ago, those two days we had together, what we did with Nathan, it feels like a dream. A weird and wonderful dream. Wonderful, not only because they happened, but because they made me draw again. That night inspired one of my best drawings to date.

I know sometimes you feel guilty about me pledging to be your online submissive again, guilty because of your situation and because you don't know when or if we can ever be together again. I told you it was okay, and that I was happy to have you in my life in whatever way you could manage. But truthfully I do think about what it could be like, what our life could be like if we were together.

I was thinking of the treatment I have to do for Stefan, 'a man comes home from work'. This is how I imagine us.

You call me from work.

"Pet, I'm leaving in ten minutes. I want you naked, on your knees at the front door when I arrive."

"Yes, Sir."

You know how that makes me nervous. Sometimes you ask me to be waiting naked for you, but usually in a room, in bed. You know that I worry that people might see in when you open the door. But today your voice is gruff, urgent. I don't argue.

When you arrive home I am as you commanded. You close the door behind you and immediately drop your things to the floor.

"Come over here, my slutty little girl. And take out my cock."

I am giddy with nervous excitement. I have no idea what you are thinking, what you will ask for. Will you want me to suck you? Stroke you? Fuck you? I am breathless with anticipation.

With shaky hands I undo your jeans and reach into your shorts. My hand is met with your already fully engorged cock. It is hot and hard and pulsing. My heart leaps into my throat. You've been thinking about something. And you want it very badly.

"That's right, little girl. I've been thinking about you," you say in a husky voice. "Push my pants down like a good girl."

I comply. I wait for you to tell me to take you in my hand or my mouth, to turn around or lay down so you can take the body I've pledged to you. But you don't. Instead you grasp your cock in one hand and push the other through my hair around to the back of my neck, pulling not roughly but firmly, so that I am forced to look up at you.

"You know what I was thinking about at work today? I was thinking about last night. When I was fucking you. And that slutty little pussy of yours was so eager, it couldn't stop clenching. It made me come when I wasn't ready for it yet. Do you remember that, pet?"

Oh, I do! Of course you don't talk about how you'd denied me for a week before. How you'd teased me for an hour before we started fucking. How my pussy was so primed and slick and desperate to be filled that I was practically gagging with how badly I needed you inside me.

You go on. "I started thinking about that at work. And I couldn't concentrate." You begin stroking your cock, slow and steady. "See what you do to me, little girl? See what your eager little cunt is responsible for? Do you see why we have to train you not to be quite so slutty?" Your voice is getting harsher, I can see your neck tense up, I see your eyes hazy with lust as you look in my mine and keep stroking. "I bet you want my cock inside you right now, don't you?" Oh god, you know I do! But all I can do is breath hard with your cock inches above my face, your hand still clutching the hair at the nape of my neck. "Well you're not going to get it today, little girl. You have to learn patience. You have to learn you don't always get what you want." Your words start to catch as you get close. "Today what you get is my cum, not inside you like last night, when you sucked it out with that greedy cunt." You're breathing hard now, stroking more urgently. "Look at me, pet." I look right in your eyes. In them I see my own desire reflected back at me. "You will have my cum when I give it to you. Where I give it to you. And right now," you pant, "I want to come on your pretty face." You let out a groan. I feel hot, wet splashes across my cheek, on my neck, over my forehead, into my hair. I groan too, and my eyelids flutter closed as I bask in the feeling of being showered in your essence, of you marking me, of being yours.

When you're done you sink down beside me. You take my face in your hands and gaze at me covered in your come. You move in and kiss me, slowly, passionately, the taste of you in my mouth, in yours, our tongues swirling together. You reach between my legs and sink your fingers in my wetness. There's no hiding the way you've taken me has me just as worked up as last night, especially since I was not allowed an orgasm then either. "Naughty girl, still so eager," you mutter onto my lips. You scoop out my juices and bring them to my face. Now I can smell you and me. You push your fingers in my mouth, pulling in some of your cum from my face and our smells and tastes are all over me as you kiss me more and more.

"Go clean up now, little girl," you say, standing. I am breathless and excited and so aroused. You see the shine of desperation in my eyes and you smile widely, knowing how denying me when you've been sated makes me weak with desire for you. "And I'd like a nice hot tea, when you're done."

"Yes, Sir," I whisper.

OCTOBER 2

I guess the situation between me and Sir and Nathan is … complex. I was talking to Delia about it at dinner tonight.

"Charlotte, you look amazing," Dee said.

"I feel amazing."

"Wow, you are positively glowing. If this is what having two men in your life does for you then I'm going to have a talk with Sebastian." She dunked a fry inside her panzerotti, scooped out some sauce with it and ate it. "I'm glad we're back at Gino's again. Japanese just didn't feel right."

"Delia!"

"What? You wanted those noodles again? They looked like a pile of worms. You didn't touch them."

"I don't mean the food. I mean the 'two men' comment. I don't 'have two men in my life'," I said, doing air quotes with my fingers. "And I love udon. I just wasn't feeling well that night." I grinned at her.

"Oh come on, look at you. You look like the cat

who ate the proverbial canary. Edward, Nathan. One, two. Math don't lie, my friend."

"One: Nathan. Edward isn't here," I said. I looked at my phone. "And he's married."

"But he was here," Delia said, staring at me with her intense hazel eyes. "He must have managed to get away from his duties at home somehow because you told me he came here. But you still haven't told me what happened."

I thought about months before, at Gino's, not that long after I discovered Bill and Ashley together, when Delia accused me of playing with fire because I'd talked to Ashley about a threesome. Was what happened with Edward and Nathan like that? Was I playing with fire? Would Delia think so?

"I don't know if I can talk about it, Dee," I said.

Dee was quiet a moment. Then she said, "Because whatever happened included Nathan?" I didn't respond.

"Charlotte," Dee said leaning over the table towards me. "You can tell me things. You know you can. We've been friends since we were six, for Chrissake."

"But what about what you said before. About what happened with Ashley?"

"I apologized for that," Dee said. "And anyway, that was different. Anybody could see things weren't good with you and Bill, with your marriage. Adding Ashley into the mix was just asking for trouble." She sighed and fiddled with her napkin. Then she looked up. "But now you are free of that. And I'm so happy for you, Char. I've never seen you like this. You look like someone has switched a light on inside of you."

"I feel like that!" I gasped.

"I can tell," Dee said. "So you don't have to be feel shame about who you are or who you want to be with. Not with me."

Shame.

I thought about shame then, and what it had meant so far in my life. Shame had forced Bill and I into a marriage that was a farce, that was doomed from day one. Shame had derailed me from finishing my BFA, when thoughts of what Daddy had said and done infected my ability to be creative. Shame had plagued me with those dreams. Shame over what Edward and Nathan and I had done together that night had sent me spiraling into the dark place that Bill found me, when I couldn't go to work, couldn't eat, couldn't get out of bed.

Dee was right. I had to stop being ashamed.

"You were right, Dee, about his wife," I started. "She is young. She's our age. It's just like with that guy at your work you were telling me about, Eddie." I pushed fries around on my plate. "They had only been married about two years when it happened."

"Wow," Dee said. "And he's been with her ever since?"

"Yeah," I said. "He said Xander's been great, really understanding. They let him work from home most of the time. And he said he's okay in the day to get out and go to client meetings for a couple of hours here and there. He said she sleeps a lot in the day. It sounds like she's on a lot of medication." I looked down. "But he said it's really difficult at night. She's got this problem with her sleep cycle so she's often awake." I took a drink of wine, blinking. "He said the time he was here when I first met him, her mother was in town. He had the conference then so, since his mother-in-law was going to be staying with Anne, he lined up some other meetings as well and stayed for the month. When he got back he found out his wife nearly died when her mother was out for a late dinner one night and Anne tried swallowing a whole bottle of sleeping pills." I paused, staring past Dee's shoulder and thinking about Edward's face as he told me the story, the creases between his eyebrows, his mouth a stoic straight line. "Now he's more afraid than ever to leave her at night."

Dee and I were both silent. I thought about what else Edward had told me, about before the stroke, how they used to be together. She was the one who got him interested in power exchange, he said. She brought out his inner dominant. One night, he said, he tied her up and spanked her. He said it was so hot they both got completely swept up in it. He untied her so that they could have sex. She called him "daddy" and while he was fucking her she sucked her thumb.

I think I looked uncomfortable then and he noticed. He said, "I know, I never thought I would be into anything like that. It sounds like it has something to do with actual parents or with children or something. But what I realized in those moments was that it wasn't anything like that at all. It was all about feeding the opposing sides of dominance and submission, of pushing one side up and the other down. It's all about power." I thought about the pig tails then, of how that made me feel so little, so small, so submissive to Sir. He was so right.

It was a week after that night that his wife suffered the stroke.

Afterward he kept reading more and more about power play and BDSM. At first he said it was a way for him of still feeling connected with her, of keeping those moments between them alive, since after the stroke she had little interest in being intimate with him. He said he kept waiting for her to come back to him. But she just never did.

"They sleep in separate rooms," I said quietly. I thought for a moment. "I thought things were lonely for me. With Bill."

More silence.

"But he did come here," Delia prompted.

"He did," I smiled. "He got a carer to come in, gave her strict instructions not to leave Anne alone for a moment in the night time, and he just got on a plane."

I paused then and thought, as I had so many times since, what he said when he showed up at the library that day: "It had been so long since we'd talked. I didn't realize how much I relied on our communication every day until it was gone. But you closed your account, you blocked me. I told myself if you didn't want me to get in contact with you I would respect that. But I couldn't stop thinking about you. I couldn't bear the idea that you thought I was just another cheating husband, that you didn't understand what you meant to me. I didn't know how else to communicate with you. I ordered that book about stroke as a way of trying to explain my situation. I thought, at least if you knew something about how I could do what I'd done then I could live with myself. But then, when I got the notification that it came in, when I imagined you getting it and seeing my name, I had to come. I know it's not fair of me to be here. I know I can't give you what you want, what you deserve. I only have two days. I'll leave if you want me to but I just had to see you again."

I closed my eyes. "And you're right," I said to Dee. "We were together. The three of us. Edward, Nathan and me." I breathed in and out, sitting still for a moment. Then I opened my eyes and held my chin out. "It was the most intensely powerful, totally sexual, amazing night I've ever had."

"Holy ... " Delia said. "I ... I kinda don't know what to say. I want to ask for details, but that seems really tacky now, somehow."

I smiled. "I wouldn't even know where to begin." I cocked my head. "But maybe one day I'll be able to sketch something."

"Do you love him?" Dee asked

"Who?" I said, resting my head on my hand, feeling

a little worn out from the intensity of our conversation.

"Both," Dee said.

"Yes," I said. Then let out a little giggle.

"Who?" Dee said, giggling too.

"Both." I took a sip of wine. I felt a little of the stress drain away with our giggles.

"Right. But now he's back home," Dee said.

"He is. We talk almost every day on Skype."

We looked at each other softly, the fact that I was communicating daily with a man who I could never be with, an unspoken acknowledgment between us.

"Well," Dee said, raising her eyebrows at me and sticking a fork and knife back into her panzerotti. "That sounds like two guys to me. How else do you explain your 'youthful glow', shall we say?"

"Well," I said, stretching my arms upwards. "Getting proper sleep at night certainly helps," I said. "The dreams are gone and I'm drawing like a fiend. Really, I feel like I've hit my stride and things are just flowing again."

"That's great," Dee said.

"Aa-nd," I sang, "things are back to being hot as fuck in bed with Nathan and me." I smirked at her.

"Oh thank god," Dee said. "When you were slipping back into your Downton Abbey routine, you scared me. What fixed it?"

"Oh," I said taking a bite of my dinner. "It's hard to explain," I said around my chewing. "Next time. That's more than enough deep and meaningful for tonight, wouldn't you say? I'm going to finish this pie. I am starving!"

OCTOBER 6

It was so much fun today watching my little subbie pick up the books I made him put on hold: *How to Please a Woman, Sex for Dummies,* and *Premature Ejaculation and You.* I just watched with glee from the back. There was no missing his flaming red face as Mel checked him out. She even had a little smirk too. She and I will have to have yet another chuckle at my boy's expense later.

When he came back to tell me his task was completed I made sure I gave him a little peek of what was NOT under my skirt before he left … .

The look on his face said his balls are just aching with all the cum I'm not letting him release.

OCTOBER 7

I just got off a Skype call with Sir. Quickly. What I mean is, he had to quickly say goodbye. And for the very first time, right before he hung up, I heard … her. Anne.

It's amazing it hasn't happened before now, when I think about it. And here's the thing: it's one thing to learn about Anne from Edward, to discuss her with Dee, to talk about Edward's wife in the abstract, almost as though she's a character on a TV show. I feel compassion for Anne the same way I felt compassion for poor Lavinia when Matthew was so clearly in love with Mary on Downton.

But it's another thing entirely to be talking to Edward and then to hear his wife's voice from in the room there with him, the voice of the woman whose husband you've had inside you, the voice of the woman whose husband, truth be told, you want to steal away.

And then my feelings for Sir and my feelings for Nathan got all jumbled up. I think I'm okay with it one minute and the next it seems all wrong.

What am I doing? Can I keep doing this? How can I feel this way about Sir when he's married. And how can I reconcile those feelings with my relationship with Nathan?

OCTOBER 8

Dear Charlotte,

Last night when you called and confessed to how you feel about Edward I found it difficult to explain my feelings. So I thought I would send you a letter, a written one, like when I was tree planting.

I know you love Edward, Charlotte. I've known for a while. It's hard for me to describe how it can hurt me and scare me but how it also inflames me and excites me. The night you told me you were with him was so erotic for me. And the letter you wrote me after ... oh my god! I've read that letter hundreds of times. Sometimes I can't even touch myself when I'm reading it or I'll make myself come.

The night we were all together in his hotel was so intense, scary, sexy and amazing. Seeing him pleasure you, watching your gorgeous body contort and writhe with him inside you, witnessing the look on your face, was breathtaking. If I didn't know you loved him before that night I definitely knew then. To be honest there was a point that I wasn't sure if I was going to be okay. When you humiliate me it pushes me down, down, I feel like I'm going into a hole. But then you looked at me. I don't know if you are aware of it but you have this look. It's a look that let's me know that I'm your boy, that you're going to take care of me. That you love me. You gave me that look that night when we were with him. When he was inside of you. And the combination of that look of love and care when I was feeling so vulnerable and the fact of him pleasuring you at the same time was what made that night the most erotic of my whole life.

I know I told you before that I didn't need the Domme/sub part of our relationship. Remember when I said I didn't need that? Well I was wrong, Charlotte. I do need it. We never talked about it, but our sex life went flat after that. I know, it was still loving and fun ... but not like it was. I know you felt it too. I never told you this but I've been reading a lot about guys that like the stuff I do. Cuckolds. When you tease me you are giving me what I love. I love the attention. I know that seems strange to some people because it's negative attention but you know I love it. You know it, Charlotte! And for me, I feel that what goes on between us in those moments builds our connection with each other.

So please don't stop. Please don't end things with Edward. Please don't stop teasing me. Please don't stop giving me what I love, Mistress.

Yours always,
Nathan

OCTOBER 9

Last week Nathan was telling me that he was not confident in his essay writing skills. So I thought up a fun task. I told him I would give him a topic, a title for his work, and he was to submit an essay to me. He needed to research it properly and provide his source materials, just as he does for his school assignments. Then I would provide comments and suggestions and give him a grade.

Why Mistress Makes Me A Premature Ejaculator

Whenever I participate in sexual activity with my beautiful Mistress, I ejaculate extremely quickly. Why is this? First we must examine the condition. What is a premature ejaculation (PE)? No one can agree on an exact definition.

One definition says that premature ejaculation is a condition in which a man ejaculates earlier than he or his partner would like him to. When I am with Mistress I always ejaculate earlier than I would like to.

Your Mistress also agrees that it is far too soon. Laughably, humiliatingly, too soon.

Another definition says PE is the condition in which a man ejaculates before his sex partner achieves orgasm in more than fifty percent of their sexual encounters.

More than 50 percent, little boy? How about 100 percent of your encounters with me?!?

Some reports define premature ejaculation as occurring if the man ejaculates within two minutes of penetration.
NB: Often you don't even manage penetration.

But all of these definitions rely on subjective response, anecdotal reporting, and the variations in what each person would like to happen during sexual activity. And the fact is, there is great variability in how long it takes men to ejaculate and in how long their partners would like them to last. Even early research demonstrated some confusion. The famous Kinsey report, while relying on the definition as ejaculation within two minutes of penetration, went on to report that 75% of adult men ejaculated in under two minutes in at least 50% of their sexual encounters.

Cf. Your track record of lasting under two minutes in 100% of your Mistress encounters.

As a result, in more recent research on human sexuality, researchers have begun to form a more quantitative evaluation of premature ejaculation. They have assessed the time between the very beginning of penetration to the very beginning of ejaculation. In men in stable heterosexual relationships, ages 18 and up, the average time was 5.4 minutes. Men who were circumcised lasted longer than those who were not by an average of about 45 seconds. And while the average was easy to determine, the range from shortest to longest was quite significant. In the study, 26% of the men lasted ten minutes or longer, while 14% of the men lasted less than 3 minutes, 20 seconds. The longest time was 44.1 minutes. And the shortest was 30 seconds. *Very good research, little boy! It's good to know you can do some things right.*

Extremely rare? Sweetie, you have never lasted anywhere close to 5.4 minutes with me!!!

What does that mean for me? Well, the average time was 5.4 minutes. It is extremely rare that I can last 5.4 minutes with Mistress. So by every definition and calculation, I come much too fast with Mistress. I haven't "gotten used to it" or "grown out of it" or made any other significant progress in lasting longer.

Aw, poor baby. No you haven't. You just can't hold your little messes in your balls. But you're trying! It's so cute.

This should be good.

The following are strategies I've used to try and combat my issue. I've tried to slow down during masturbation to learn to last longer. I've tried distracting myself during sex by thinking about very unexciting things. I've read articles online about different techniques for slowing down an ejaculation and I've tried many of them: stretching my balls, slapping my cock, pinching the head of my cock, squeezing the base of my cock. None of those helped.

Maybe try turtle sex?

You think slowing down to turtle speed will help? That's cute but I may get a little frustrated during sex when you're fucking me like a turtle.

Hmm, I've done the cock slapping but maybe I should try some of these others for you, huh little boy?

I've tried the old "start and stop" method: completely stopping all movement during intercourse to calm down and even pulling all the way out as a means of stopping and calming down. But every "stop" is followed by a "start" and that almost always results in a spill. I've even purchased a fake pussy—a male masturbatory aid—to practice. But truthfully, it is very tight and makes me want to come even faster than a real pussy.

when I let you!

I just want you to know I laughed a lot when I read that.

Aw, was it tough writing that one down? giggle.

So none of that has helped a great deal. I still make subtle shifts in my body all through foreplay to avoid Mistress's leg, hand, or other parts of her gorgeous body from rubbing up against my cock and getting me even closer to the edge before I get to put it in. I still start struggling with the first plunge inside her pussy again, in an attempt to slow down. I always imagine I can lower the stimulation and last a lot longer but it doesn't seem to work. *Sure doesn't!*

on the occasions when you even manage to get that far stopping and starting, going slow, squirming around to change angles and sensations do you see me sigh and roll my eyes during all these silly little movements that are supposed to be like fucking?

It isn't just me. Lots of guys struggle with this, apparently. There are millions of web sites devoted to "solutions" for PE. Often there is even a Premature Ejaculation Calculator to help you figure out if you are one of them.

You should say 'us' here, love. You are definitely a member of this little club!

Does that make you feel better, sweetie? Th you're not t only pathet little quick comer out there?

Some aspects of play and control are appealing to me, but the bottom line is I cringe and wiggle and pant and moan and do everything I can to hold back longer every single time. And on almost every occasion, it just doesn't matter. I'm totally spent, empty, done, limp, useless, flaccid, pathetic while Mistress is still getting warmed up.

Laughing again!

are they, now? Isn't that amusing! Only some? I would say all!!

And to answer the question 'why,' what is it about Mistress that makes me lose control? I'm not sure. Something about the way she looks at me, the things she says, her gorgeous body, just make me not able to control my own little cock. It touches a part of her that feels good and I'm almost instantly wanting to come and end the fun

sometimes we don't even have to directly touch it, do we, little boy?

Oh honey, don't you know, the fun is just beginning for me then! Your pathetic little fast squirts just spell the beginning of the tirade of humiliation I'm about to rain down on you. That is so much fun for me.

I know, I see you doing that, little boy. It amuses me greatly.

I haven't learned to control my little cock the way a real man does. I haven't learned not to squirt it all out far, far too early. I have a weak little penis.

Thank goodness Mistress is amused and entertained by my lack of stamina and is willing to work with a little premature ejaculator to find other ways to pleasure her ... since my cock just won't do.

Bibliography

'Premature Ejaculation.' *Wikipedia.* Wikimedia Foundation, Web. 7 October. <http://en.wikipedia.org/wiki/Premature_ejaculation>.

'Supplemental Content.' *National Center for Biotechnology Information.* U.S. National Library of Medicine. Web. 7 October. <http://www.ncbi.nlm.nih.gov/pubmed/16422843>.

'Intravaginal Ejaculation Latency Time.' *Wikipedia.* Wikimedia Foundation, Web. 7 October. <http://en.wikipedia.org/wiki/Intravaginal_ejaculation_latency_time>.

http://penthousestore.com/couples-and-toys/masturbators/penthouse-reg-pet-cassia-riley-pussy-stroker/14730/ *Is this where you got your little toy from? 'laughing!'*

Staff, Mayo Clinic. 'Definition.' *Mayo Clinic.* Mayo Foundation for Medical Education and Research. Web. 7 October. <http://www.mayoclinic.com/health/premature-ejaculation/DS00578/DSECTION=treatments-and-drugs>.

'Premature Ejaculation Calculator - Detect Premature Ejaculation Symptoms.' *Premature Ejaculation Calculator - Detect Premature Ejaculation Symptoms.* Web. 7 October. <http://www.calculatorslive.com/premature-ejaculation-calculator.aspx>.

Humiliation Phone Sex: Small Penis Humiliation, Verbal Humiliation and Cuckold Humiliation. Web. 7 October. <http://www.phonehumiliation.com/index.php?action=show> Shall we make you pay to be humiliated next time, for example, when too I'm busy getting fucked properly by Edward?

B+ Overall this is well researched and edited. The one omission that stands out to me is that you failed to mention the completely humiliating occasions when you are not even able to manage penetration at all. Was that just too difficult to write about? Aw.

I'm not sure that you answered the question, why it is that you can't control yourself for Mistress. I am giving you a decent grade anyway for your research efforts and writing quality. I don't think you need to be so concerned with your essay writing skills, little boy. As this essay demonstrates, your lack of ability lies elsewhere.

OCTOBER 15

Sir and I haven't discussed what happened that night when Nathan and I both went to his hotel room. We haven't talked about Nathan at all. But tonight on Skype … we did.

It started out rather innocently. I was telling Sir that I've been working steadily with Stefan on the book and the sketching has been going really well. Then I mentioned that I needed to do one more sketch, a sort of finale, and that I wanted it to be the hottest yet.

"So what are you thinking, pet? Do you have some ideas for what you might draw?" he asked.

"I think so, Sir." I looked at him and then blushed

and looked down.

"Aw, does your idea embarrass you? I'm intrigued." Even on Skype I could see his eyes glimmer.

"Well, really, you already know about it. The fantasy, I mean. My fantasy," I said.

"So what's all the blushing for then, my pet? What is this idea?"

"It's the one I told you about when we first met, while we were sitting in the hotel bar." I looked up at the screen from downcast eyes. "Do you remember?"

"Of course," he said, smiling. "I wouldn't forget my pet's most prominent desire."

I giggled and pulled my hair over to cover my face.

"I'm still waiting to hear what all this embarrassment is about," Sir said, that sexy eyebrow raised.

So I told him. I told him how—perhaps because of what happened during his last visit—my secret ultimate desire had morphed into something else. It now included Nathan.

OCTOBER 19

I told Sir I am having trouble with that final sketch. It needs to be completed by November 15th and, for the first time since I was having the dreams, it isn't flowing for me. He suggested that writing down something about that ultimate fantasy might help.

I had the original fantasy for so long. Saying it in words, speaking it aloud to Sir that night, our first night together, was so difficult. Writing about it now, now that it has changed to include the men who I love, to include Sir, to include Nathan, is so much harder … but also so much more intensely alluring and sexual.

For the longest time it was just a faceless man dominating me, denying me. Then that man became Sir. Sir tying me up, Sir licking me, Sir telling me to be a good girl, to be still, to not come. Now it had changed again. Instead of Sir licking me there was Nathan. And instead of binds to hold me down, there was Sir. The rule was still that I was not allowed to come. That

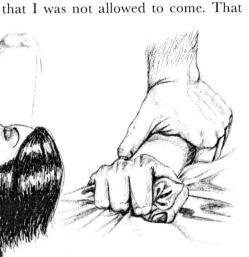

was the rule for me, anyway. Nathan had a different rule. His rule…was to make me.

OCTOBER 24

Oh god. I'm screwed. I can't do it.

I will have to call Stefan and tell him one of their other artists will have to finish the final sketch for me. I know that's crazy, not just because I've left them little to no time to create the work, but mostly because, how can I want someone else to finish what I now think of as *my* book? What will it look like when the final sketch is obviously the work of a completely different artist?

But I don't know what else to do. My heart is broken and I just cannot make the work come.

I thought I could handle it. I told him I could. But the more communication I share with Sir, the more our bond grows and the harder it is that I never get to feel his touch. Yes, I want Nathan, my sweet boy, my horny little plaything who I love so dearly. But I guess I'm greedy. I also want Sir.

Sir spoke about her in our last conversation. (Our *last* conversation. Will it really be our last?) I try never to ask about her, about his wife…about Anne. It felt to me like an invisible boundary I instinctively knew I had no right to cross.

But when we were on Skype two nights ago, even though I knew I was a complete bitch for doing it, even though it seemed callous and wrong, even though I couldn't believe the words were coming out of my mouth as I said them, I said them. I asked. I asked the thing that was the most unfair, the most cruel. I asked the impossible. I asked what I knew he would say no to.

I asked him to leave her.

"Sometimes I think I could," he whispered, his voice cracking. "But then…I'll catch this glimmer. Of her.

I'll see her. The *real* her," he said, his eyes all glassy. "I don't mean physically. She lost interest in her appearance right after the stroke so she never does her hair or her makeup or puts on pretty clothes like she used to." I started crying too, then. "But I mean in her eyes. It'll be a certain look she gives me or a smile. Sometimes she'll even crack a joke that will be just like something she used to say. It doesn't happen very often. Especially not in the last few years. But in those moments I think, there you are, my love! There you are." Tears rolled down his cheeks and he looked straight at me. "And then I hate myself for ever thinking I could leave."

I hated myself too, then.

But I didn't retract my plea.

I told him I didn't want him to answer then. I just wanted him to think about it. Really think about it. And then give me his decision.

So I gave myself the day yesterday. Just one day. And I let myself daydream all the things I didn't let myself imagine before. I imagined introducing him to Dee, to Mel, to people in my life. I imagined him picking me up from work. I imagined talking to him and being able to touch his face. I imagined kissing him at the end of a long day.

I imagined making my fantasy with him and Nathan come true.

I imagined it not being just some silly drawings in a book. I imagined it all being real.

I gave myself a day to do this. And I loved it. I loved every fucking second of our beautiful imagined reality.

I gave myself a day. One day to fantasize...before he told me what I knew he would.

"I'm sorry, pet," he said quietly. "I just can't."

"Then please don't call me that anymore," I said. "Please...don't call me at all."

I held up my hand. I held it up to the web cam. I made sure my ring was visible, the beautiful ring that I loved so much, that symbolized not only my submission but his dominance and how there was a little of each inside the other, making it work so well together. The ring he bought for me, that he engraved with our names, *For pet, your Sir*, that I promised not to remove until we agreed my submission was over. I looked in his eyes.

I think we could both see it was over.

I took it off. "Good bye, Edward," I said.

November 16

To: Charlotte Campbell <ccampbell@pp-lib.com>
From: David Burlow <dburlo@xanderpublishing.com>
Subject: Artwork

Dear Ms. Campbell,

I am in receipt of your artwork via courier last night and I have to tell you, I am most pleased. This is indeed the pinnacle piece of the book. Thank you kindly for your efforts.

What's left now is to ensure that everything is tied together within the framework of the story. I know you've worked with Stefan to loosely weave your artwork into a cohesive piece but if you have any final thoughts on how best to accomplish this I am very happy to hear them.

Sincerely,

David Burlow

NOVEMBER 18

To: David Burlow <dburlo@xanderpublishing.com>

From: Charlotte Campbell <ccampbell@pp-lib.com>

Subject: Re: Artwork

Dear Mr. Burlow,

I am so happy to hear you are pleased with the artwork. Thank you for asking my thoughts regarding weaving the story together. In fact I've had a brain wave. It takes the book in a different direction than I had been discussing with Stefan but, not only would the artwork you've approved not have to change, I would also be able to provide you with a complete manuscript.

I think it would be best if I could meet to discuss my idea with you in detail. Kindly advise when you would be available. I look forward to hearing from you.

Best,

Charlotte Campbell

NOVEMBER 30

Delia joked with me tonight that we're going to have to start meeting for dinner at *La Bohème*, the fancy French place in the city, once my book is a huge success.

"Yeah right, Dee. Like that's gonna happen."

"Come on, Char. Think big!"

"I am." I grinned at her. "I meant I'm obviously not going to have time for dinner with you anymore, once I'm all famous and shit."

She threw a fry at me.

"Okay, time to dish! Last time I talked to you, you were panicking and saying you absolutely could not get the final artwork done on the book. Now you've done it and they're launching it in the new year! What happened? I've been waiting over four weeks to hear the story."

I shrugged, smiling and blushing a bit. "I know, I'm sorry, Dee," I said. "I've been a little busy."

"I'm sure you have," Dee said, giving me a wicked stare.

"Besides," I said, shaking my head. "As if you don't know what happened."

She rolled her eyes. "Well yeah, I guess I know generally. But come on, Char! I need details. This is the third trip he's made now. Is he here for good this time? What did he say when he showed up? What did Nathan say?"

I finished chewing my mouthful and took a swig of red wine.

"Enough stalling already! Tell me about when Edward came back." She picked up her wine glass and settled into her side of the booth, obviously preparing for something lurid and titillating.

"Actually," I said, "it's not like what you're expecting." I sat back in the booth too. "When he showed up at the cottage it was terrible. Heartbreaking. Edward is always very calm and in control. But he was a mess that day. I'd never seen him like that," I said. "He told me the turning point for him actually came from Anne's mother, Julie."

I remembered how he'd looked that night he showed up, when he explained what happened, what Julie had said. He gave me and Nathan, who was with me in the cottage at the time, one hell of a shock when he came to the door in a taxi at about ten o'clock at night a few days after that last Skype call. That last call had really rocked me so I thought I would have been thrilled to see him, over the moon, beside myself. But he shocked me. He looked like such a wreck. He was unshaven, unshowered and unkempt. His eyes were so red and puffy it was hard to believe he could still see out of them.

"Julie called me," he croaked. "After our Skype call that night." He shut his eyes a moment. "She said she wanted to talk about Anne. I was so upset about us, I didn't want to talk to anyone." But he did talk to her.

He described their conversation. "I guess her realization came when I had her come out to stay with Anne the last time I visited you. She said, 'I can see now that Annie isn't the same person anymore. I can't imagine how hard it's been on you.' Then she apologized to me for not coming more often years ago." He sighed. "I did used to feel so angry at her for not being around, for not spending more time with Anne so that she could understand what she was going through." Nathan and I had brought Edward inside, into the bedroom, had settled him on the bed and he sat there, legs outstretched on the mattress, his back propped up against some pillows. I could see how he was grappling with all of his emotions. "Then she said, 'It's time for you to live your life now, Ed.'"

He looked at me, finally seeing me then. "She told me to live *my* life." He took in a big gasping breath. "So I couldn't stay," he said. Then he started to cry. "But I can't believe I left." And then he cried in earnest.

"Wow," Delia said, when I'd finished telling her. "Permission from the mother in law. That's big."

"I know," I said. "But he was still such a mess that week."

The cottage only has one bedroom but the couch pulls out so we set him up there and that's where he stayed. For a week he didn't move from there. Nathan and I took turns bringing him food that he mostly didn't eat, and cups of tea that he'd drink half of and then forget about, leaving them to sit and turn stone cold with little circles of milk thickened in the middle of the remaining pale brown liquid.

At the end of the week he got a phone call on his cell. Up until that point when he got a call he would look absently at the number and then let it go. His boss at

Xander knew he was having personal issues though, so he wasn't getting a lot of calls. But this one he picked up.

Nathan was at school so it was just the two of us. I had gone into the bedroom to give him some privacy but eventually I heard him call out to me so I went back in and sat on the edge of the pullout.

"That was Julie, Anne's mother," Edward said. He'd told us that, before he left, he had managed to get her to come back and the two of them had briefly discussed finding care for Anne. "She said Anne's doing okay, all things considered." He sighed and scratched his head. "There's a care facility not too far away. I asked Julie to call and she said they may have a space opening up."

"That's good," I said.

"Of course Anne doesn't want to go there," he said, his face contorted with emotion. "Who could blame her? I mean, it's not a hospital. It's a nice place. But still…" I sat next to him, stroking his back and feeling so useless, so guilty.

"I asked Julie if she was remembering to put Anne's clothes out for her everyday on the bed, the way I'd shown her. If you lay them out backwards, you see," he said, looking at me earnestly, "she gets confused and frustrated and can't get dressed on her own." He grimaced and I thought he was going to cry again, but he didn't. "Julie didn't remember what I was talking about. I was so annoyed with her. I told her I was going to come home, that it was all a mistake." He was breathing hard then, clenching his fist against his thigh. "But then," he said, his breathing slowing a bit, "then she told me that if the care facility didn't work out, that she was going to stay there with Anne. Move in." His eyes watered and he was looking past me, out the window, but I could tell he wasn't taking anything in. "She told me that I'd done enough."

"He was better after that phone call," I said to Dee.

"By the end of that week he was going in to work at Xander again. He's really lucky that he can easily work from the office that's here. It's actually better since it's the head office."

Delia looked genuinely happy. "I'm glad for him. The poor man's been through a lot."

"Me too." I grinned. "Especially because, once things started to turn around for him, that's when they turned around for me too."

"Are we finally getting to the good part now?" Dee said, sitting up and taking another sip of wine.

"Well, let's just say that what ended up happening between the three of us inspired that final piece for the book." I smoothed my napkin out with my fingers and smiled at her sweetly. "And just in the nick of time!"

"Yes, yes," Dee said, a glint in her eye. "Go on!" But then she put her hand up. "Oh wait! Before you get to that, tell me how you've ended up getting the writing cred on this thing too."

"That's easy," I said. We continued eating while

I explained how the idea came to me in a flash, that we could simply use my diary to tie all the sketches in together. "They all came from here anyway," I said, patting the diary that I had sitting on the table beside us. "And it's all done. Well, almost."

"That's so cool!" Dee squealed. She waved the waiter over and soon we both had two full glasses of red. "Okay, okay. Now. Tell me. What went down with the three of you?" She grabbed up her glass again. "And speak slowly. I don't want to miss a bit!"

I reached for my glass too and assumed a casual air. "Hey," I shrugged. "You'll see that final sketch soon enough. And you know what they say about what a picture's worth."

"Oh come on! You're not even going to dish on the deets?" Dee crossed her arms and sulked. "I'll tell you what else is worth a thousand words … a thousand words!"

"Well actually," I said, looking askance. "That's why I say 'almost.' There is just one more thing they are waiting for from me to complete the book." I fiddled with my glass. "Just like you, they want the words to go with the picture. That final one."

"You're going to write about what happened with the three of you to include in the book?" She looked incredulous.

"I kind of have to. It completes the story." I took a swallow of wine. "And hey, you haven't seen the rest of what's in it. After what I've already written, I might as well." I blushed but smiled.

"Well, Charlotte Campbell," Dee said, looking at me with what I dare say was admiration. "This is a long way from the woman who was panicking over just one sketch that included a person who might resemble her."

"I know," I said. "But you were right."

"I usually am," she quipped. "What about this time, though?"

I laughed. "About creativity. About artists sketching what they feel passionate about. You said I should embrace it. Well...I am."

I looked at Delia then, my dear friend, who was like a sister to me. "None of this would have happened if it weren't for you, Dee."

"Hey, don't pin your crazy sex life on me!" she said, laughing.

"No, I mean the book, silly," I said. "You're the one who gave me this diary for Christmas last year, for my sketches. You encouraged me to start drawing again. If it weren't for that I wouldn't have had anything to submit to begin with. And I certainly wouldn't have a whole year of my life to share."

We held up our glasses and we toasted each other. And then we toasted Xander Publishing's first book in their *Red Ink* imprint.

DECEMBER 1

So now I know, as I write this, that there is a 'you.'
You, the reader. You will be reading this.

Are you like Delia? Do you want to know what
happened once Edward was back, really back, once he was
himself? Do you want to see how Nathan participated? Do
you wonder what they did to me? What we did together?

Is the picture enough?

Or do you, like Delia, want the thousand words too?

It happened on a night about two weeks after
Edward came back to us. Nathan and I had eaten dinner
together and Edward had been out with clients. We didn't
know what time Edward was going to be back and, to be
honest, we were a little preoccupied.

I had Nathan's hands tied up behind his back.
Although I was fully dressed, Nathan was clad only in little

briefs. They were white with blue edging on them and I'd made him purchase them one day when we saw them in the store because I thought they looked like something a little boy would wear. "Little boys who don't know how to fuck properly," I whispered in his ear as he handed his card over at the checkout. With his new muscled abs and bulky biceps the juvenile looking briefs stood out even more and I giggled as I tucked the top band gently underneath his balls, exposing all his sensitive flesh to me. I began stroking his quickly stiffening shaft.

"Don't get too excited too quickly, little boy," I cooed in his ear. "You've got to hold your orgasm for me and show me what a big man you are." I was sitting behind him on the couch, cradling him with one arm while I stroked with the other. I bit his ear lobe softly and said, "You can show me, can't you?"

In no time his rod was a rigid pole and he was moaning and begging while I continued to tease him. He begged to see my body, to touch it, to lick it, to be allowed inside me and, of course, to come. I told him he wasn't allowed any such thing, that he was far too eager and unskilled with his teeny dick to be granted access to my body. That just made him moan louder and tell me he needed a break from the touching.

I was giggling when the door opened. And in stepped Edward.

Usually Edward dressed casually to go into the Xander office, often something like khaki pants and a collared shirt. But because he had dinner with a client this night, he was wearing a suit. It was charcoal gray as was his tone on tone patterned tie and his white dress shirt stood out crisply. It was the first time I'd seen him dressed in business attire and, cliché as it was, I could not stop my heart from skipping a beat. I gazed at his stern look and the flecks of gray in his dark hair. He looked so commanding and so fucking sexy.

"Well, well, what's going on here?" he asked as he walked into the room and set his briefcase down. "Somebody is having fun with her little plaything, it would seem."

Nathan and I looked at each other and, crazy as it was, I felt overwhelmingly like we were two pets who'd just been caught lying on the furniture when they knew it was forbidden. Nathan sheepishly tucked his dick back into his briefs.

Edward loosened his tie and ran a hand through his hair. "Charlotte," he said, and I immediately lowered my head and peeked up at him from under my brow. Just his tone did that to me. "I need to speak with you in the bedroom, please."

I followed him to the bedroom feeling all the more like his little puppy. He opened the door and motioned me in, shutting it behind us. I was already excited from teasing Nathan—playing with my little boy never failed to make me clenchy and slippery, although I hid it all behind a cool facade—and now, alone in the room with Edward and not knowing what was on his mind, I was aroused and nervous and submissive all at once.

He looked at me wordlessly at first. Although I was fully clothed his gaze made me feel exposed. I lowered my eyes, waiting for him to speak. Though I had not submitted to him for months I felt that familiar heart beat start up again: *make me, make me, make me.* I didn't even know what it was I wanted him to make me do. All I knew was how good it felt to step outside of my comfort zone with Sir. For Sir.

Finally, he spoke.

"Charlotte, remember when you wrote me that fantasy, 'A man comes home from work?' I nodded slowly, remembering, my pulse quickening. "Well, tonight I've come home from work to you." He stared at me, letting his words sink in. My eyes went glassy for a moment as I thought about just what it took for him to be here with me like I'd fantasized about. "And just as in your story, I've been thinking about you. Distracting thoughts, while I was with my clients. But instead of what you wrote about in that particular story," he paused and swallowed, "I've been thinking about your ultimate fantasy." He stepped toward me, ran his hand through the back of my hair, grabbed a hand full at the base of my neck and tilted my head up to him. He leaned down close to my ear. "There are things I need to do to you," he growled. "But first," he said, loosening his hand from my hair, "a question."

He guided me to sit down on the edge of the bed and he sat facing me. "I asked you that first night we were together in my hotel room if you wanted to submit to me." I felt my eyes light up as I remembered our first night together and my first night of submission. "Tonight, I'm asking you that question again. But not just for one night. This time, Charlotte—" He paused, looking into my eyes intently. "This time, *pet*, I want you to be mine … indefinitely."

My body was thrumming with submissive desire and I could barely speak. But he knew. He asked for my ring and I hastily went to my things to grab it out of its special box. As before he had me put it on and kneel, only this time Sir could put the ring on for me and when I knelt, I knelt before him. To kneel before him with his ring adorning my finger and knowing I was his was a pleasure that went beyond simply the erotic. It was all encompassing and it left me breathless and buzzing. Then he reached for my hand and brought me onto his lap. He kissed me long and slow and soft and whispered in my ear that I was his baby girl and that he would always take care of me.

"Now Charlotte, I'm going to have a shower," Sir said, patting me on the bum so that I rose and he began undressing. "You need to go back out there and speak to your little boy." He was down to his boxers when he said, "Ask him if he would like to play with us." He raised his eyebrow. "This time not sitting in the corner and watching, but actually participating."

My heart kicked into overdrive. Nathan and Sir? Together with me at once?

"Yes, Sir."

"If he would like to join us," Sir went on, "he also needs to address me as 'Sir.' You need to ask him if he has any hard limits with regard to our play." We discussed a few more of the fine points before I went out there to speak to Nathan. Considering the letter he wrote me I guess it should not have surprised me at all that Nathan readily agreed.

"Now Nathan," Sir said, when he'd joined us out in the living room again, "what was it that my little pet was doing with you when I walked in."

"She was teasing me, Sir ... "

I thought it might be strange to hear Nathan call Edward "Sir." Instead, it seemed not only fairly natural, perhaps because of their age difference, but also undeniably hot. For me, anyway, and both Nathan and Sir seemed unphased.

" ... And not letting me come," Nathan concluded.

"Isn't that interesting," said Sir. "I also, you may have heard, like to play such games with my little pet." Sir eyed me meaningfully. "Let's do that now, shall we? You'll play with us. You'd like that, wouldn't you Nathan?"

"Yes, Sir."

Sir had us all go into the bedroom where he said he'd explain 'the rules.'

"Unlike what I imagine your Mistress was doing with you, I'm going to give you the chance to earn your orgasm." Sir eyed Nathan's still hard cock, the head poking out of the top of his little boy briefs, and bulging testicles. Nathan turned the brightest shade of red I'd ever seen a man turn as Sir said, "You look like you could use one." Sir went on. "You will lick your Mistress. You will try your best to make her come. If you succeed in providing this pleasure to her you will have earned your orgasm, to be executed in any way you choose." At this news Nathan really did look like a boy who'd just gotten his Christmas wish. "Now pet, your only instruction is not to come." Just the thought of how this game could play out was making my pussy start to throb. "Succeed and your reward is the knowledge that you've pleased and proved yourself to me, your Sir, that you have control." Sir knew that my mantra, "My pleasure is to give Sir pleasure," I took to heart. I loved to please him. "Fail, little girl, and you will be punished."

They both proceeded to undress me and just that, having my two lovers' four hands running over me, removing clothing and grazing my skin with their warmth, left me dizzy and gasping. By the time I was naked on my back with Nathan's head between my thighs and Sir holding my arms firmly behind me I was already melting into a puddle of Charlotte flavored goo.

Then Nathan gently parted my pussy lips with his fingers. "Just kiss her there softly," Sir told him and Nathan did as he was told. His soft lips felt exquisite on my sensitive little nub and I moaned. "That's it," Sir said. "Just make out with that little clitty and show your Mistress what she means to you with your mouth." With that kind of encouragement Nathan gently lapped and kissed and rolled my clit around his tongue. I gasped and sighed. "Keep your legs wide open, little girl," Sir warned, tightening his grip on my arms and reaching forward and giving my right nipple a little pinch.

"Oh!" I called out. He reached over to pinch the other one too, and soon he was going back and forth between them, plucking them into little hard peaks of engorged flesh. The combination of this stimulation with Nathan's mouth between my legs had me starting to buck and gyrate. "Oh Sir!"

"Yes, pet?" Sir said, in a voice so calm it was maddening. "If you are getting close to having a little cummie then I will give you a chance. You can tell me and I will consider getting your little boy toy to pause a moment while you get a hold of yourself."

Nathan's tongue continued working my button. I felt my legs start to shake. "I'm getting close, Sir!" I called out.

He chuckled. "Nathan, your Mistress, for all her toughness on you, seems unable to control herself in this moment. We need to give her a little break." Nathan obeyed. "Did you know, Nathan," Sir's voice, from behind my shoulder, was smooth and controlled, "Charlotte's told me how much she enjoys your oral efforts. Did you know that she loves it?"

I looked down at Nathan and he smiled more than a little shyly. "Yes," he replied.

"Did you know that she often struggles to maintain her control when you have your mouth on her? Did she tell you that? That's how much she loves your tongue."

"Sir!" I cried. "You weren't supposed to—"

"Shush now, pet. I'll decide what I'm supposed to do."

Nathan's eyes were lit up like stars. "May I?" he asked, looking at Sir.

"By all means," Sir said.

When Nathan put his mouth back on me it was with a renewed effort. Knowing how much his licking affected me seemed to spur him on, as Sir must have known it would. It was true, Nathan had learned my pussy so well and his tongue often had me teetering on the brink in no time while I tried to maintain my cool. Now his fervor had me back there easily.

"I'm close, Sir!" I called out again.

"Is that right, pet?" Sir said while Nathan persisted in his efforts.

"Yes!" I cried, more urgently.

"Hold it for me, pet."

I tried. I tried relaxing my muscles, willing my body to be calm, but Nathan's talented tongue fluttering on my clit could not be ignored. As soon as I relaxed my pussy muscles just clenched back up again involuntarily, gearing up for the glorious release I could feel was around the corner.

"Sir, please! Please make him stop!" Begging for

the exquisite attention on my pussy to stop was a torturous mind fuck because, god, did I want it to go on and on.

"Nathan, a rest again, please."

I sagged back against Sir's chest, panting, still feeling his one arm tight around my two behind me.

"Nathan, put your fingers inside your Mistress, please."

"Oh Sir, no!" I said. "You know I can't take that."

"You will try for me. Won't you, pet?" I looked at him with pleading eyes but nodded. He looked at Nathan. "You may resume."

Nathan's fingers shunted in and out of my cunt, stretching me, filling me. He sucked my clit into his mouth and tongued it steadily. My body tensed almost immediately. I could feel my orgasm loom.

"Sir, make him stop! I can't hold it, Sir!"

"It must be hard to concentrate on what you're doing, Nathan, with all this yelling," Sir said, his voice like silk.

"Sir, please, please!" I wailed, as Nathan began tonguing harder. "Please, I can't—"

My eyes bulged as Sir grabbed the lower half of my face, his palm firmly planted against my mouth. I tried to yell but only a muffled noise came out. Sir had me completely pinned, restrained, and now I could no longer talk. Nathan's ministrations were putting me over the edge and there was nothing I could do about it. I felt submissive and helpless and somehow, confusingly, ironically, so so free. "You take it, little girl," Sir whispered in my ear. "If you can't hold your come it's only because you're such a horny little—"

I howled out from behind Sir's hand as Nathan's tongue and fingers sent me crashing over the edge. My body thrashed and twisted and Sir held my upper body while Nathan grasped on to my lower, making sure he sucked every last spasm from my pussy.

These two men, my Dom, my sub, held me and forced my orgasm right out of my body. They sent me into the most exquisite bliss.

After, of course, the punishment and reward had to be doled out. Sir said it would. Nathan chose to be in my mouth. I was on all fours sucking him and as he watched Sir administer my punishment—a sound spanking on my ass while he fucked me hard from behind, telling me what a naughty, slutty little girl I was—well, my poor little boy, couldn't last long with that kind of display in front of him. He spurted down my throat after about a minute. But even Sir wasn't long after him. Just before he came, he gave one last crisp smack to my butt cheek. He said it was for having such a wet pussy that it fairly sucked the cum out of his cock, as he groaned loudly and thrust hard against me.

I lay there afterward, Sir's wetness between my legs, the taste of my sweet boy in my mouth, sandwiched between the two of them in my bed. Here I was with two men whom I loved and desired, their bodies warming me from either side. And I felt loved and desired right back.

Did I feel shame? Shame for loving them both at the same time? I'd spent so many long, lonely nights. So many years. I'd cried myself to sleep more times than I cared to consider pining for this feeling of being desired. God only knows how often I felt broken. Maybe this is what it took to fix me: two men's desire. Or maybe I just fell in love with two men and this is how we'd chosen to express it.

Maybe I just didn't care.

Because for the first time that I could remember … I felt truly happy.

December 20

Probably just so that I don't get too big for my britches with the book launch coming up next month, Pig Face has me scheduled to work in the Dungeon today. Good times.

Today it doesn't even feel like the Dungeon! "Ah, Fritz, my old buddy! We had some times, didn't we, Fritzy old pal?" I said, and wondered why I was suddenly talking like Jay Gatsby. "How about I give you a little pat on the exception bin? Or hey, I'm feeling a bit naughty. How about on your induction belt, hmm? That's where you really like it."

That's what I was saying when Pig Face walked in. But instead of giving me an earful, she just turned around and left.

Ha.

The Times

PIG FACE'S REIGN OF BIBLIO TERROR ENDS!

That's right. She's not so high on her horse ever since Xander, on Edward's suggestion, arranged with the branch manager to have the book launch here. All those times she gave me grief for sketching in the Dungeon and now they've made a book of my work that's bringing publicity right here to Parkdale Library. I'll make sure I sign one copy just for her.

Well, can't sit around and gloat all day. Better see what Fritz has for me.

HARDEN, EDWARD *Polyamorous Relationships: Making it Work*

Oh, Sir!

JANUARY 7

A portrait of the artist stepping out of her comfort zone.

A portrait of the artist embracing her passion.
A portrait of the artist … without shame.
Happy fucking New Year!!

CPSIA information can be obtained at www.ICGtesting.com
Printed in the USA
LVOW10s0135100614

389236LV00001B/1/P